CONTENTS

Raging Storm	1
Prologue	2
Chapter One	3
Chapter Two	37
Chapter Three	64
Chapter Four	91
Chapter Five	118
Chapter Six	139
Chapter Seven	160
Chapter Eight	184
Chapter Nine	206
Chapter Ten	223
Chapter Eleven	246
Chapter Twelve	260
Chapter Thirteen	285
Chapter Fourteen	305
Chapter Fifteen	322

Chapter sixteen	348
Chapter seventeen	374

RAGING STORM

The Legends of Endonia

Written by S.B.C Davies

PROLOGUE

After the war that had ravaged the world of Endonia, a tepid peace had been forged and the world began to heal. In this world, a young man finds himself torn between two words yet accepted by neither.

He is a Half-Breed. Unwanted and alone, he has fought his entire life just to survive. And yet, despite it all, this young man will one day be the catalyst for Endonia's future.

He will find a way to unite Endonia once and for all, or see to its ruin.

CHAPTER ONE

The City of Ryu

He had no real name. All he had been given in way of identity was a letter. 'A' was classed a Half Breed. Born half Pangarian and half Kaligan, A was an outsider to both races from the moment he was born. An outcast no one wanted or could accept. The Kaligans were of pale skin and white hair. Their bodies were tall, and their ears pointed high. The Pangarians were amber-skinned like the sky at dawn with hair of vibrant colours and rounded ears.

The two races were the majority of the known world and had been bitter enemies for as long as anyone could remember. Old rivalries and resentments against one another had expanded the ever-growing gap between them until it became a chasm so large any attempt to unite them seemed futile. Other races called the world of Endonia their home but their marks on history were vastly overshadowed by the unending hostilities between the two majority races.

Half-Breeds such as him would never be accepted. Being half of each feuding race had only brought him pain. He was either too much or too little for either race to deem him part of them and the other minority races were uninterested in such a person. He had the height of a Kaligan though his ears were not as pointed. He also had the Pangarian skin of amber and had a thick mop of pale blue hair. As such A struggled to make a life for himself. It was only when A reached twenty-five summers old did he dare take a stand against the disdain thrown against him for the crime of being born. He was twenty-five when he dared take his life into his own hands and attempt to live, not just survive.

In the City of Ryu was where it all started. Where A's life would cross with another in the most unlikely of ways. Ryu was a city where you could easily get lost in. Carved into the mountain that sat towering above the western plains, its colourful houses and buildings could be seen from miles away in the bright daylight. The city itself was built atop itself, buildings almost stacked atop one another in towers that reached the mountain peaks. The winding roads within the city were maze-like with massive staircases leading to different parts of the city. It was joked that if you weren't a citizen of the city, good luck in finding your way out.

The city was separated into three sections. The highest section was dubbed the Meridian Quarter. Named after the iridescent seas found on the other side of the continent, it was where Ryu's most elite and wealthy resided. Below that was dubbed the Guild of Trading, where most of the city's merchants and traders set up shop. Bringing exotic treasures and fabric from all across Endonia. Or so they claim. It was also those of moderate means who lived and worked, not nearly as wealthy as those above their heads but enough to get by.

In the lowest section, un-ironically dubbed the Dark Quarter. Where the city's seedy underbelly was in control and not the city's Garrison. Riddled with crime and filth swept away from above, the section had practically become a ghost town in the last few years. Those in residence of the Dark Quarter were those who were criminals themselves or those who could not afford to move lest they become homeless. It had gotten to the point where city officials had a second entrance constructed so those entering the city could avoid the section altogether, further dividing the city.

On the threshold between the Dark Quarter and the Guild sat a small tavern called the Wilting Rose. Painted red for its namesake, the Wilting Rose was known for its cheap drink and connections to Ryu's infamous red lantern district. This meant the tavern's regular clientele was less than stellar compared to those on the upper levels. There was hardly a week that went by when someone wasn't thrown out by the tavern's owner due to fighting or illegal acts. That day was like any other for those inside the tavern.

The sun had just started to set on what had been a warm spring day and the tavern was already bustling. Even though Ryu boasted about the city's welcome of all races, tensions still ran high between the Pangarians and Kaligans. Especially in places where alcohol was flowing, and inhibitions were low. Thankfully, it seemed the promise of a night of good drinks and entertainment was enough to quell tempers even for one night inside the Wilting Rose. It was also partly because any rowdy patron was quickly made silent when they met the owner.

The owner was named Tomska, an unusually temperamental Borgan. Borgans were half-giants, their incredible strength and foreboding height matched only by their gentle hearts and whimsical singing voices. Though seen as forces to be reckoned with, Borgans rarely, if ever, chose to fight. They were pacifists in every sense of the word. Tomska was clearly cut from a different cloth. His greenish-grey skin turning purple at the drop of a hat and thundering at whatever poor employee had angered him that day.

"Milta!" Tomska yelled despite the Pangarian bartender only a few feet away from him "Table five needs refills!"

The green-haired man was already exhausted, sweat dripping down his forehead. His shift had been manic from the get-go. He had walked into work only hours before to a filthy tavern and a kitchen in chaos. The day previous had been his day off so he had been unaware of the madness that awaited him.

He had learned that the previous night, a fight had broken out between the cooks and the front staff which led to fists flying and the kitchen's large cauldron somehow ending up embedded in the wall, ram and liver stew left splattered across almost every wall. The two offending employees were fired leaving the tavern understaffed, meaning Milta had to be both Barman, Server and cleaner. Just to add more stress, it was a night when the tavern was exceptionally busy.

Still, Milta plastered on his signature smile for his boss whose temper was already hanging by a thread "You got it, Boss" he responded, taking the bottle Tomska set out and walked over to table five that was situated under one of the tavern's windows.

Two Kaligans sat at said table. They sat across from one another; both sets of greyish blue eyes set intently on the cards in their hands. As Milta walked closer, he saw they were playing Empress Flush.

It was a game where you had to get all four Empress cards before the other. Now Milta didn't consider himself to be someone who cared about differences. Granted as a Pangarian himself, he wasn't fond of Kaligans on principle. However, tips helped pay the bills, so the small pile of coins made him hopeful of some extra money coming his way if he played his cards right. No pun intended.

"Here you are, Sirs," he said refilling their glasses with red wine "Will there be anything I can get you? We just had a shipment of smoked bore crackling if you're interested"

One of the white-haired Kaligans shook his head. "No, thank you" He then smirked at his friend across from him before setting down his hand in a flourish. Four Empress cards. "Well, would you look at that? I win again"

His friend whose long hair was tied up in a bun, threw his cards on the table in a huff "Why do I keep playing this stupid game with you?" the other simply chuckled, pulling his small pile of winnings towards him smugly. "Come on. Another round"

Milta coughed "Well if you need anything else, I'll be at the bar" He was about to leave when one whistled for him to stop. The Kaligan then tossed him two silver coins with a nod. Milta thanked him and went back to work. He did bite the coin to ensure it was indeed real silver and not a fake. He'd fallen for that one before.

On the other side of the tavern, tucked away in one of the dimly lit corners sat Trisk. Trisk was also a Kaligan travelling from the bitter north in search of his one true love. Knowledge. Trisk was a Scan, one of the few Kaligans to take up such a position. Scans were researchers, teachers, scholars, and most importantly, keepers of knowledge. Scans were people who willingly gave up their previous lives in exchange for learning all Endonia had to offer. The more senior Scans of which Trisk was one, would seclude themselves away in their Great Libraries to fully immerse themselves in their craft. Rarely would they leave their sanctuary after doing so.

Trisk was different. He held the same thirst for knowledge as the rest of his compatriots and wanted to learn all there was to learn, but Trisk had what most Scans didn't. An undeniable wanderlust. He had become restless and unchallenged back home, becoming bored with his everyday life. So, one day out of the blue, Trisk packed his things and set off. Scans travelling by themselves were few and far between in recent times, so Trisk was determined to make his journey meaningful. He was going to make history as the discoverer of some great unknown find he could claim for himself.

So far that plan had yet to be successful. In the year he had spent travelling, the most he had been able to uncover were two sought-after books that his library back home had yet to acquire. Not exactly something to write home about. Other than that, Trisk had yet to find anything that piqued his interest.

Of course, he knew that great finds would take time and effort to accomplish, but as time went on, he couldn't help but worry that he made a mistake leaving home. He had travelled to Ryu in hopes that the bustling city would give him a lead on something extraordinary. Which is how he ended up in the Wilting Rose, nursing a mug of ale staring down at his bare-paged journal and feeling rather sorry for himself.

The ancient black wooden door to the tavern opened allowing the last remnants of daylight to enter. The hooded figure walked inside, floorboards creaking under his boots. The man wore an old yet well taken care of cloak that hid his body and appearance. He was met with the smell of freshly poured drinks and the sounds of drunken chatter and singing. The man paused at the threshold, scanning the inside of the tavern with shadow-covered eyes, before taking a seat at one of the empty tables. He sat there for a while, silent and almost motionless. One hand on the table clenched in a fist.

Eventually, Milta walked over to take his order. Usually, he would wait for people to order at the bar to make things easier for himself. Now the earlier rush had died down for a bit, he figured he'd go take his order while he could. "What will it be?"

The man didn't look up "Just a small ale" he responded, placing three coppers on the table for him.

"Coming right up," Milta said taking the money.

Since it was a small order, Milta was back within moments with the drink. He set it down before the man. "Here you go. Anything else?"

The man shook his head "No, thank you"

Milta regarded him with a nod then left. The hooded man left his drink untouched for a moment, his head swivelling back on forth scanning the room. Seemingly satisfied that no one was paying attention to him, he reached up and pulled down his hood. He shook his head slightly allowing his light blue curls to fluff up a bit after wearing the hood for so long. He brushed a loose lock of hair back, revealing a semi-pointed ear. Seeing this, Trisk all but dropped his empty glass in shock. He truly could not believe what he was seeing.

He continued to stare unseen as A downed his drink in one go. A usually chose to keep the hood up when in populated areas but the day had been a warm one and he needed a moment to breathe without the stifling hood surrounding his head. Also, by the looks of those inside the tavern, everyone was either too drunk or too preoccupied to cause him any trouble. That is, till his light blue eyes met with Trisk's grey ones. Trisk waved at him excitedly like a child would to their favourite person. Meanwhile, A simply slumped back in his seat.

Trisk wasted no time in hurrying across the room to A's table, sitting himself down across from A with a beaming smile "I could hardly believe it when I saw you. I've never met one of your kind before" A frowned, pulling his hood back up. Trisk immediately said "Wait, no. That's not what I meant. It's just… Well, I'm a Scan, you see?" he said showing the golden Scan pin that was pinned to the collar of his shirt. "I'm on a research expedition, as it were, to discover something unseen till now"

A stared at him unimpressed "I'm not an oddity"

"No, but you are a rarity" Trisk pressed, the excited grin never leaving his face "I've basically spent the last year travelling the continent and I've never come across a Half Breed. You may be one of a kind!"

Trisk was met with a confused and offended stare "Was that supposed to be a compliment?"

"Well, yes... No? No. I'm sorry" he apologised under the Half Breed's intense stare. "I just get so excited about things, you see. Can't really turn it off" Trisk pulled out his journal and quill, placing it on the table between them "May I please interview you?"

A blinked "Excuse me?"

"Just for a little while" Trisk promised "We have hardly anything on the lives of Half Breeds such as yourself and it would truly be something if I could bring a genuine report back home" He looked at A hopefully "Please? I've been gone a year and I have next to nothing to show for my troubles. Everyone back home will see me as a joke if I return empty-handed. Please?"

He wanted to turn the Scan down for self-preservation alone. However, that pleading pathetic look in Trisk's eyes swayed him. A let out a tired sigh "Fine. Half an hour"

"Two hours" Trisk offered

"One hour and you're buying the drinks" A countered

"Deal!" Trisk agreed instantly "Bartender!" he called over his shoulder "Two tankards of your best mead and keep 'em coming!" from the bar, Milta shouted back a confirmation for his order. "Ok, first things first. I need your name"

Already, A clammed up at the question. Waves of nerves overcame him in an instant. He breathed out a harsh breath, steadying himself. "I don't have one"

That made Trisk pause, his ink-dipped quill stopped on the first page. He looked at the Half Breed before him curiously "You... You don't?" He asked sounding far less sure of himself than before.

A shrugged "Nobody ever bothered to give me one. I go by A"

"As in the letter A?" asked Trisk again. When A nodded, Trisk was openly in shock "That's um... Damn," He hadn't anticipated this. Of course, he had suspected the life of a Half Breed wouldn't be an average one given the rampant hostilities between races, but to learn the man sitting across from him didn't even have a name? Well, Trisk suddenly felt very awkward. He coughed, moving to sit upright in his chair as Milta came over with their drinks. A kept his hood up and didn't look Milta in the eye. Trisk noted that down. "Um... May I ask which parent was which race?"

Again, A shrugged "Couldn't tell you. Never knew them"

Trisk winced at his foolishness. Only two questions in and his interview was already in the outhouse. Still, he jotted that down too, wanting to catalogue everything A told him. "So, where did you grow up?"

Just like before, A had little to say. "Around" was his only answer. Trisk frowned seeing A grip his tankard tensely, hand slightly trembling and his head bowed forward to hide his face further. The Scan realised his question must have stirred up some rather uncomfortable memories for A. Growing up as an orphaned Half Breed couldn't have been easy, that much Trisk was certain of. He wrote down A's reaction in shorthand before continuing.

"What about your diet? What are your favourite foods?" Trisk asked hoping a change of direction would ease the other.

A glanced up, his amber-skinned face surprised at the question "My favourite food?" he repeated and Trisk nodded "Huh. No one's ever really asked me that before. I guess it would be Endon berry cake? I had it once years ago. It was pretty good"

"Endon... Berry cake..." Trisk muttered whilst writing it down, adding his own theory as to why the food was A's favourite. He paused to take a big swig of his drink then pressed on. "Alright, next question. So, as a Half Breed, what side do you consider yourself more like? Pangarian or Kaligan?"

A answered simply "Neither" He sipped at his drink thoughtfully "I was welcomed by neither, so I consider myself neither. Are you done?"

"Huh? But we agreed on an hour"

"And I have changed my mind" A responded, tossing a couple of coins down on the table for his share of drinks as he stood from the table. "We're done here" A then secured his cloak, gathered his bag and began walking to the exit.

Trisk called after him "Hey, wait a second! I have so much more to ask you!" but A was already out the door "Damn it" He quickly gathered his things and hurried after the Half Breed. He knew deep in his gut that this was what he had been looking for. That once in a lifetime find. How many of his colleagues back home could say they managed to find a Half Breed? Some of them didn't even believe they existed.

So Trisk was all the more determined to follow after A and learn everything there was to know about him.

Exiting the Wilting Rose, Trisk looked around for A only to catch his hooded figure walking down one of the paths leading to the Dark Quarter. Trisk wasn't the most athletic of Kaligans having spent most of his adult life in a library, but nothing was going to stop him from going after A. Trisk sped off after him, clutching his satchel close so as to not lose it. A had already managed to get a few steps ahead of him so Trisk had to pick up the pace to keep up. "Wait a moment!" he called after him once more and once more A ignored him. "I'm sorry if I offended you. I was just so curious!"

Trisk continued to follow A into the lower streets where the Dark Quarter truly lived up to its name. Most of the section barely saw daylight given the construction of the new bridge above. The lack of natural light and dark shadows made the buildings seem like they were not just towering but looming over those passing by. The darkness playing tricks on the mind, making the faded colourful buildings much more menacing than what they actually were. Despite his growing unease, Trisk kept his stride up. He was nothing if not determined and maybe a little stubborn.

Finally, A came to a stop to speak to someone. By now Trisk had followed him into one of the lowest streets of Ryu where the roads were dust and the houses mere shacks compared to the buildings that saw sunlight. Without stopping to catch his breath, Trisk walked forward and grabbed A by the shoulder "There you are. Look, I'm sorry for –" When the other turned around, Trisk realised then he had been following the wrong person. When leaving the tavern, he had mistaken someone else in a similar brown cloak for A and had followed him without checking. Trisk was now standing deep within the Dark Quarter, being smirked at by someone completely different.

The man pulled down the hood of his cloak, revealing he was a Pangarian with deep red hair and vermilion eyes. He was taller than most Pangarians which aided in the mix-up of identity. "Well, well, well. What have we here?" he asked crossing his arms "Now what's a well to do Kaligan doing in a place like this?" Trisk glanced down at his clothing, silver threaded black silk and fur-padded boots, and gulped nervously.

"Uh – Um..."

"Don't be afraid. We just want to talk" Suddenly, at least six other people were appearing from the shadows "I believe introductions are in order "I am Jask, a humble swordsman. Pray tell what might you be, good sir?"

Trisk couldn't tell if he was being genuine or just messing with him "My name is Trisk. Scan of the Redencon Great Library, fifth class" he announced, forcing his voice not to tremble with nerves.

Jask then looked delighted "We have a Scan! Just what we've been looking for lads!"

Trisk gulped "Oh dear..."

The red-haired Pangarian took a step forward towards Trisk, one hand out as if to grab him, only to stumble back and shout in surprise when something hit his chest. His pale blue shirt was now soaked in dark red liquid dripping onto the floor. "What the –?" he wondered noticing the remnants of a glass bottle at his feet.

"Don't just stand there, you idiot" came a familiar voice. Trisk's head snapped upwards to where the voice came from. To his surprise and relief, A was above him crouched on one of the shack roofs. "Run!" Trisk didn't need to be told twice. The Scan bolted back the way he came, ignoring the aching in his legs as he ran up numerous paths and staircases. He kept running up, lungs screaming and heart pounding until he made it to the closest market in the Merchant Quarter.

Dozens of people were wandering the market giving him ample cover. Trisk wheezed harshly, hands on knees as he tried to catch his breath. He received several odd looks from passers-by when they saw him in such a state.

Someone's hand tapped his shoulder and Trisk nearly jumped out of his skin. He swung his fist out of instinct, narrowly missing A who had just caught up with him. "Whoa!" A ducked out of the way at the last moment "Watch it, will you!"

"A? Oh, thank the Creators" Trisk sighed "For a moment I - I thought you were..."

"I take it you don't visit Ryu often. Everyone knows you don't go down there by yourself unless you're looking for trouble" said A looking at him like Trisk was stupid.

Trisk glared at him half-heartedly "I thought I was following you!" he defended himself. "Wait, how did you know where I was going?"

"Because after I left, I realised I left something behind on the table. I came back only to find you following a stranger into the lower levels. I couldn't exactly let you get mugged down there"

That surprised Trisk. After their short conversation/interview, he assumed A would be steadfast in ignoring his existence. Which is why he had been so adamant in following him. Trisk had much more to write about A, that much he could bet on. "Hey!" a sharp voice rang out. Both men turned to find Jask walking intently towards them, his brow furrowed, and clothes still soaked from A's interruption. "There you are"

Trisk backed away "H-Hey now, I don't want any trouble"

The Pangarian came to a stop before them, giving them a confused look "What? I don't want to hurt you"

Both A and Trisk side-eyed each other "What?" it was A's turn to ask "Then, why did you follow him all the way up here?"

"Because he's a Scan and I wanted to ask his help" Jask explained with a nonchalant shrug "We were sent documents from a new client, but they're written in eastern Endon. None of us can understand them. We heard Scans are good at translating stuff like that"

Realisation hit the two men hard. Trisk hadn't been in danger of being mugged at all. It had all been a misunderstanding. "Ohh...But if that's true then why did those other men circle me like that?"

Jask had the decency to at least look embarrassed. Rubbing the back of his neck awkwardly, Jask spoke "Yeah, sorry about that. We were kind of desperate and didn't want you to leave without helping us" He shot them an awkward crooked smile that was missing a tooth.

Trisk couldn't help but huff a laugh at the absurdity of it all "Well, we're sorry about your shirt. I'll translate it for you. In fact, my friend here will tag along to help" A snapped his head to look at Trisk in disbelief.

"What? I didn't agree to this" he whispered to Trisk in a harsh tone

"Whatever they pay me, I'll give you. Deal?"

With a nearly empty coin purse and boots in need of urgent replacement, A felt obliged to agree. He let out a weary sigh "Why do I have the feeling I'm gonna be stuck with you?"

❈ ❈ ❈

The trio returned to the Dark Quarter, following Jask to avoid the more unsavoury of characters living there. Just because Jask wasn't the threat they anticipated, didn't mean that the fabled Dark Quarter was a safe place to be. Jask showed them on the way down which paths to travel with care and which to avoid altogether.

"Don't worry though. Those rumours of a beast hiding in the shadows down here aren't real. Mostly" that did not help soothe Trisk's increased heart rate or A's nerves being on edge. When they eventually made it to Jask's ramshackle home, it was a visible relief to the two non-natives of Ryu. "Well, come on in. Make yourselves at home" Jask said, unlocking the door to let them inside. A took a moment to take in the house. It was a rickety shack in all sense of the word. Its blue paint faded to the point it was now grey. No matter the poor condition of the house, he felt a twinge of jealousy towards Jask.

He followed the others inside, only to find the small building packed with at least a dozen other men strewn about doing various activities. Both Pangarian and Kaligan. There was even a Borgan sitting near the window. Trisk had the same expression, especially when they caught sight of two strongly built Pangarian men sharpening their weapons in the corner. A's hands came up and pulled his hood down tight against his head.

"Everyone!" Jask announced to the men "This is Trisk the Scan and..." Jask paused, remembering he'd never gotten the other's name.

"My assistant" Trisk lied

"Trisk and his assistant are going to translate the documents for us" Jask received a rousing cheer from his men "Leave them to their work and please, for the love of Ryu, don't frighten them. That goes especially for you, Cori" he said gesturing one of Pangarians, summerstone coloured hair pulled back into a bun and fiddling with his crossbow.

Cori rolled his eyes "No promises"

"Come on. In here" Jask said with a wave of his hand. "You can work in the room over here" He showed them to a small office like room with a table, three chairs and mountains of papers piled high to the ceiling. "The documents we need translating are on the table. If you need anything, call for Col. He'll sort you out" With that, Jask left them to it. The papers on the stained and splintering table were stacked in a messy pile. On the table were also several lit candles, empty cups and glasses, dirty dishes, and a rather fat cat dozing on while under the candlelight. Jask shut the door behind him leaving them alone inside the room.

"What have you gotten me into?" A wondered aloud, finally pulling his hood down due to the stuffiness of the room. The lack of a window certainly didn't help matters.

"It won't take us long" Trisk commented flipping through the pile of documents "I've done more in two hours back home" Upon closer inspection of the documents, Trisk barked a laugh "No wonder they couldn't understand this. This isn't just East Endon, it's East Kaligan. Complete nonsense to people down here" he glanced up at A who was still stood by the door with his back against it "You any good at translating?"

For the first time since they met, A looked embarrassed. He turned his head away, semi-pointed ears going pink under the candlelight "I... I can't read. Or write"

Trisk was stunned to silence. The thought of someone unable to read or write was unthinkable to a Scan. Even the poorest people he'd met during his travels had least the basic understanding of reading and writing. He could scarcely believe it. "Oh. I... I had no idea. I'm sorry" It seemed apologising to A was all he was doing. "Well, I could still use some company while I work" he offered with a hopeful smile. A thought for a moment before gingerly taking a seat at the table.

The hours passed with little conversation. Translating the documents were easy enough for Trisk. It felt a little like he was back home, working by candlelight poring himself over foreign texts late into the night. A was quiet though he did speak when spoken to. Whilst Trisk worked, A eventually drifted off into a light sleep with the cat curled up on his lap. The plump black and white cat purred away contently. Trisk finished as those outside began to turn in for the night. He debated on waking A but chose not to. Instead choosing to let him rest for a bit while he handed the newly translated documents to Jask.

He quietly left the room and luckily found Jask nearby. Trisk handed him the papers. "There you go. As promised"

Jask grinned "You are a lifesaver. Col, pay the man" Col appeared beside Trisk, a kind faced Kaligan several years older than him with his fair share of wrinkles and soft grey eyes. He handed Trisk a coin purse clinking with coins with a nod, saying nothing at all. Jask read over the papers but started to frown. "Wait... Wait, this can't be right" he said aloud "Are you sure this is what it says?"

"I translated it right down to the letter, as requested. Is there a problem?"

"Yes, there's a bloody problem" snapped Jask turning angry "Lord Callum is trying to stiff us! We were promised fifty silver each for that last job and he's trying to pay us only ten. Son of a Banshee!"

Trisk stuttered for a moment "That does sound bad"

"You bet it is. He's not getting away with this" Jask almost growled standing up from the table, glaring at the paper as if it had personally offended him. His head snapped to Trisk. "You have your payment, now get your friend and get out. My boys and I have work to do"

The Scan retreated into the office to fetch A and make a quick escape. He shook the dozing man's shoulder and A shot back to wakefulness, the fat cat jumping from his lap from the sudden movement. "I'm awake. I'm awake" he mumbled

"Come on, we need to leave. Now" Trisk pressed while gathering his things. The two men quickly made their exit just as Jask was ranting to his men using a litany of swear words neither man was aware existed till that point.

Now with the moon high, A and Trisk made

their way back up towards the upper streets with haste. The last thing they needed or wanted was to be accosted for Trisk's newfound payment. By then the night markets had taken over, selling goods and much less reputable services for half the price of the daytime markets.

"Well, here's your payment. As promised" announced Trisk placing the coin purse in A's hand. A looked at the purse and then at Trisk with a shocked expression. "What? I said I'd pay you and I always keep my word"

A shook his head, putting the purse away in one of his pockets. "You truly are a strange one" he commented "Well, I better get going. Sir" A gave him a farewell gesture, turning to leave and leave Trisk's life.

"Wait!" Trisk yelled finding his voice. A paused, looking back with a raised eyebrow. "L-Let me come with you!"

The Half Breed stared at him "What?" he asked in disbelief

"Just... Let me come with you. Please? I promise I won't ask any more questions. Just let me write down my observations of you. You won't even know I'm there" he prattled on trying his hardest to convince A to allow him to follow.

The Half Breed stared like Trisk had grown a second head. He let out a heavy, weary sigh, head dropping slightly. "Even if I say no, you're just going to follow me. Aren't you?"

"Pretty much" Trisk shyly admitted

A deliberated inwardly for a long moment, his face switching through dozens of different expressions and emotions, before he, at last, gave Trisk an answer "Fine. On the condition that you don't ask a single question about me. Got it?"

Grinning, Trisk agreed to the terms without question "Deal!" he said happily, shaking A's larger hand vigorously. A snatched it back with a stern frown.

"Don't touch me"

"Right. Sorry. Again

CHAPTER TWO

Journey's Start

The Gods were trying his patience. At least that's what A thought as he and Trisk made their way towards his intended destination. From the way Trisk had spoken about his travels during the first few hours after they left Ryu, A had at least expected the Scan to have at least some survival skills to have travelled the open road. He was sorely mistaken.

As it turned out, Trisk's idea of travel and A's idea of travel was the difference between night and day. Usually, Trisk would find lodging in an Inn or a Tavern which cost Coin. Coin A did not have. The first night of travelling together was eventful, to say the least.

The place where A deemed they would sleep

was a bit off the beaten path, a hidden clearing within the towering trees that lined the road. A had hung his cloak on one of the lower branches, allowing Trisk to see the Half Breed fully for the first time. He noted A's clothing was worn and patched in some places. Aside from his cloak which looked relatively new, the rest of his clothing appeared months, maybe years old. There was a small cloth bag attached to A's belt that caught his eye.

"I don't understand why we couldn't find an Inn to spend the night," said Trisk as he gathered some fallen twigs and branches.

A rolled his eyes "Does it look like I have the coin for that?" he responded

Trisk was confused "What about the coin I gave you earlier?"

Again, A looked exasperated "Either a place to sleep for the night or supplies for the next month. Inns aren't cheap"

"I could have paid" the Scan said weakly

"And tell me, what self-respecting

establishment would let someone like me stay" A asked pointing to his half-pointed ears "I was lucky no one threw me out of the Rose back in Ryu"

Trisk went quiet feeling awkward yet again. He hadn't thought of it that way. Seeing the state of the other's clothing should have been a clear sign A hadn't spent coin on himself in a long time. He muttered "Right. Sorry" then went back to collecting wood till he had a hefty load in his arms. More than enough to last through the night. "This should do"

"Hm, not bad" A quietly praised "Toss them there. I'll get the fire going" he gestured to a decently sized pile of dry leaves. Trisk did as he was told and with a spark from two flint stones struck together, a fire began to form. Trisk smiled gratefully. The sun was hanging low, and it was beginning to get too dark for his liking. He sat across from a with the fire crackling between them. A was quiet which was to be expected. Trisk found A didn't talk much while walking, barely giving Trisk a response sometimes. This did not deter him in the slightest. Trisk was if anything if not determined.

He reached for his bag and retrieved his book. Though they'd only been travelling together for a short time, he'd already filled pages on his observations of A. Granted the notes were somewhat messy since they were written as he walked, but he could tidy them up later on. As he did this, A looked past him into the quickly darkening tree line. His pale blue eyes narrowed slightly.

"What is it?" Trisk asked not turning around to see for himself

A responded simply "Dinner"

Trisk did turn around after hearing that. As he did, he saw a fuzzy grey hare hop out of the shadows. Nose twitching and black eyes blinking. Hares were fast but A was faster. Before Trisk even realised A had gotten up, A had the hare in his grip. Trisk had a look of alarm on his face and A let out a sigh. "Do you want to eat tonight, or not?" silently, Trisk nodded "Then don't look"

Sometime later, the scent of roasted meat filled

the air. The now-skinned hare was on a makeshift spit on the fire. Trisk hated to admit it, but it smelt delicious. His stomach growled making it even more obvious. A turned the hare over to roast the other side while Trisk quietly took in their surroundings. Night had fallen leaving the fire the only source of light. Shivers went down his spine hearing a distant owl let out a hoot. He wasn't made for nature, but he could endure. At least, he hoped he could

Examining the area, his interest peaked when he spotted a cluster of mushrooms growing at the base of one of the trees. He figured some sautéed mushrooms would go nice with the hare A caught. He walked over and gathered a handful of brown flattops. He was about to take a bite out of one when A smacked them out of his hand. "Hey! What the-?"

"Are you mad?" A demanded "Roundhead, you're fed. Flathead, you're dead. Flattops are poisonous around these parts"

Trisk paled "Oh…" Thankfully, A didn't scold him further. Later, both men tucked into their simple but filling meal. The meat was tender and juicy with just the right amount of flavour. While eating, Trisk braved a question "You're a good hunter. Did you teach yourself or were you trained?"

"Myself" A responded; mouth full. He swallowed "Took a while to get good at it. Spent many a hungry night before then"

"You... said you didn't know your parents-"

A interrupted him "No questions about my life. Remember?"

"Right. Sorry. I'm just curious. I'll stop talking"

Silence fell between them save the crackling of the fire. Then A huffed "I'm an orphan" he admitted tossing the bones into the fire "That's why I don't know them"

Trisk had suspected that was the case. It would be hard enough for other children to grow up without parents. For a Half Breed? Trisk could only imagine just how tough life had been. Unable to come up with anything to say, Trisk finished off his dinner and avoided eye contact with A. The next hour was spent in silence with Trisk writing notes in his book and A lying on his back looking up at the stars twinkling in the black sky. He laid on his cloak as a makeshift blanket. Trisk continued writing till he let out a long yawn.

"You can sleep" A spoke from his spot "I'll keep watch"

Trisk frowned "Keep watch for what?"

"We're camping in a forest" A responded with a raised eyebrow "You don't think that hare we had for dinner was the only creature around here" The Scan now wide awake started whipping his head around searching for any sign of danger. A shook his head at the display. "Don't worry. Most avoid open fire. Just go to sleep"

Trisk muttered "Well I'll never sleep again" while settling down to lie on his side facing the fire. It was uncomfortable, to say the least, but he soon found his eyes drifting closed and his body growing heavy with sleep. Trisk drifted off seeing the flames dance to life.

Hours later, Trisk was rudely awakened by A shouting a curse. "Stop it. Stop it, get off" A demanded. The Scan shot up from his sleeping position, half expecting A to be being attacked by some wild creature from the forest. It took a moment for his eyes to adjust to the early daylight but then they did, Trisk almost burst out laughing.

A was being attacked if being licked to death was possible. In A's hands trying to pry the animal off him was a rambunctious, tan-coloured, incredibly fluffy puppy. The puppy seemed adamant that A was its new best friend and wouldn't stop licking and pawing at the Half Breed for attention.

When the puppy nipped at A's nose, Trisk lost his composure. "Yeah, yeah. Laugh it up" A said finally pulling a squirming animal off him. The puppy was a small thing that barely fit in his hands. Probably the runt of the litter.

"Aww" Trisk cooed "He's adorable"

A set the puppy on the ground and then stood up before it could pounce on him once more.

Trisk instantly swept the puppy into his own arms, utterly besotted with the adorable creature. He'd never had a pet before, his home never allowing animals of any kind, so he was openly excited about the puppy in his arms. "Oh yes, you are so cute"

"We're not keeping him" A stated, kicking dirt onto the embers to dampen whatever flame was left.

Trisk gasped holding the dog close "What? Why?"

"We don't have the resources to look after one of those things"

The Scan glanced at him, then at the puppy, then back at him "Well, we can't just leave him here. Poor thing was probably abandoned"

A sighed "No. We are not keeping him"

Both Trisk and the dog gave him puppy eyes with Trisk wobbling his lip for good measure. A continued to shake his head in refusal. "Trisk, no. We are not keeping him"

They were soon back on the road "Just until the next town" A stated firmly as the puppy trotted beside them, black tongue hanging out as it panted. Trisk had tried to carry him in his arms, but the little pup seemed to like A more, which is why it was happily toddling along next to A.

The Scan just grinned smugly "Whatever you say. So, where are we headed? I never got round to asking you last night"

"Riven. It's a mining village about a day's horse ride from Ryu. We should be there in about an hour or two" A explained "Might as well pick up some supplies with that coin you earned"

Trisk smiled brightly "Oh, I have an uncle who lives there. We could stay the night if you want"

A glanced at him with a wary expression "You sure about that?" he asked hoisting his hood back up to cover his ears and hair.

The other man waved off his concerns. "It'll be fine. Uncle Trindle couldn't care less about the fighting going on. Plus, he loves dogs" Trisk said beaming at the puppy trotting beside their feet "He's going to spoil you rotten, Spud"

"Spud?" A questioned bemused "Out of all the names in Endonia, you went with something that describes a potato?" even the dog himself looked a bit offended at the name choice, small head upwards to give Trisk the dog equivalent of a raised eyebrow.

Outnumbered, Trisk relented "Well, what would you name him, then?"

"Certainly not after a vegetable" mused A. He regarded the pup at his feet for a short while as they walked "How about Nippy? Since he kept nipping at my face"

"Oh, and I'm the weird one" joked Trisk "How about Trinidad?"

"Ontranto"

"Edro"

"Sunford"

"Repenue"

"I don't know, Clovis?"

The puppy yipped loudly, interrupting the conversation. "Clovis?" A repeated and the dog yipped once more. Both men looked at each other before shrugging "Clovis, it is" With that settled, the three continued down the road, passing horse-drawn caravans and wagons off to morning market. Eventually, they reached the blackened gates of Riven.

Famous for its coal and ore rich mines, Riven had garnered many travellers, workers, and merchants over the years. With the mines up in the nearby hills, Riven was a one level village built with winding roads, cobblestone paths, and rickety wooden buildings. Black coal powder caked the walls of buildings and the in-between of stones on the ground. Smog filled the air blanketing the village in a thick layer of grey. A's nose twitched at an unpleasantly familiar scent.

"Well, this is… something" A announced sounding unimpressed "You sure your uncle lives here?"

Trisk nodded "Of course he does. I used to spend winters here as a boy. Though it wasn't always like this" He was the first to step through the gates "Well, come on then. I'll show you around"

Standing at the threshold, A glanced down at Clovis who sat patiently at his feet "I'm not carrying you" Clovis then wined the way only a puppy could. "Oh, don't look at me like that. You aren't that cute" another more pitiful whine. Moments later, Clovis was sat comfortably in A's jacket, buttons done up so he wouldn't fall out. "Don't get used to this" muttered A as he caught up to Trisk.

He found Trisk not too far ahead, the other having stopped at a stall that sold a curious array of crystals and ore deposits. A made sure to keep his hood up so as to not gain any unwanted attention. Trisk was fascinated by the pretty rocks the merchant was selling. He waved A over to look alongside him. "What do you think? Blue or purple?"

"Your friend has a good eye for crystals. Good for health and vitality" the seller; a haggard old woman with white scraggly hair, leather-like skin, a black splattered apron, and weathered hands smiled.

A took one look at the array of products on the

cloth covered stall and said to Trisk "They're fake"

The old woman took offence "I beg your pardon?"

"How can you tell?" frowned Trisk

"I just can. Look" A picked up one of the purple crystals Trisk had taken interest in and easily split it in two, showing the inside was hollowed out. "See? Easy to miss if you're not careful"

The woman was now flustered at getting caught. Red in the cheek with worry in her eyes. "Please, don't tell the local Garrison," she asked quietly "It's hard enough to make a living at my age"

Trisk shook his head "It's alright. We won't tell anyone. Right?" he asked A with a firm look. A agreed with a silent nod. The woman smiled relieved and then placed one of the smaller crystals in Trisk's hand.

"As a thank you"

She waved the three of them off. Trisk took a closer look at the crystal he had been gifted. It was smaller than the others, green in hue that sparkled in the dim sunlight. Its edges were also less jagged than the others that were on the table. He hummed curiously. "Pretty" he said simply, placing it into his bag. He then pointed out one of the larger houses in the village. "There's my uncle's house. Come on, I'll introduce you"

The Half Breed followed if hesitantly. Avoiding shoppers and traders alike, they reached the door of the house. One of the few buildings built with brick instead of wood but it still suffered the same blackened staining as the rest of the village. Trisk knocked on the door and waited for a response. The door opened to reveal a Pangarian woman with thin rosewood-coloured hair and freckled amber skin. Trisk was openly confused "Um... hello?"

"What do you want?" she questioned with a sneer "We don't want your kind in this house"

"Charming" A commented sarcastically

Trisk coughed awkwardly "Sorry. Isn't this the house of a Mr Trindle Eisor?

With an annoyed grunt, the heavy-breasted

woman spoke "You're a bit late. The old codger died years ago" With that, the door was slammed shut in their faces. Trisk backed away a bit, face contorted in bewilderment.

"You ok?" asked the Half Breed

"I... have I been gone that long?" Trisk whispered. He wound up sitting on the hard cobblestone path with his back against the wall of the house out of sight from the door, head hidden behind his knees. A was unaccustomed to shows of emotion from others. Still, he was compelled to sit beside Trisk, placing Clovis before the Kaligan to entice him to stop hiding his face. It worked and Clovis began licking Trisk's face as if in sympathy.

A began to speak "Are you alright?"

Trisk exhaled slowly as he petted Clovis for comfort "It's just... I had no idea he died. I know I've been gone for a long time, but I thought I'd least be sent word when someone died"

"How long have you been gone?"

Trisk continued to pet the dog in his lap "I joined

the Scans when I was twelve, so... fifteen years. I write to my family as often as I can. Why didn't anyone tell me?" A couldn't answer. The other man sighed again "Maybe they didn't want me at the burial. Wouldn't be the first time" With a final sigh, Trisk clambered back to his feet. "Come on, local Tavern is this way. I need a drink"

※ ※ ※

If the Wilting Rose had been a hotbed for ruffians, it was nothing compared to Riven's only tavern. As the only place in town to get a decent drink, Fern's Hall was packed to the brim with drunken miners just off shift and other members of the community. Unlike its outer appearance; which was kept clean and free of coal power, the inside was a stark difference.

The inside was as dark and filthy as the coal mines themselves with only a scarce number of windows to allow light in. The floors once oak brown now plastered in black boot prints from the miners, and glasses hardly ever washed as dark fingerprints were left on them without care. Sat in the corner with a flagon of mead in hand, A watched with raised eyebrows as not one, not two, but three separate fights broke out at once egged on by drink and lack of self-control.

Fern himself, the owner and namesake, did next to nothing to quell the aggression. Clovis was kept securely on A's lap who was more than content nibbling on some roast crackling. Meanwhile, Trisk downed his drink like it was going out of style. His fifth in as many hours. A took a sip of his own drink. "Well, this is something" He took a glance at Trisk "You should probably slow down"

Trisk gulped down the last of his drink then exhaled loudly "Barmaid, keep 'em coming!" he yelled to the bar where a frazzled sunrise orange-haired woman was working. A shook his head to the barmaid in hopes she wouldn't bring over another drink. She did anyway and Trisk tossed some coin on the table for her. "Aww, what a cute dog" she commented "Is he yours?"

"I guess" A answered with a shrug

"You know what?" Trisk suddenly exclaimed "I think you're looking at this the wrong way"

That got A's attention. "I am? About what?"

"You know, everything. I think you're actually better off than me. No -" he paused to hiccup "No family to disappoint you. No need to play perfect..." Trisk laid his head on the dirty table and groaned a sigh "You're so lucky..."

A begged to differ but chose to say nothing on the subject. Trisk was drunk and not thinking clearly. Though the words stung, A tried not to take offence. If he took offence with every insult or comment thrown his way, A would more than likely be in prison by then. "What a lightweight" he quipped and Clovis ruffed along with him. Luckily, whatever disagreements that had caused the multiple fights had either been sorted or quelled as the tavern had calmed down significantly.

Now instead of fighting or arguing, there was

joyful if out of tune singing from some and the laughter of others. By that point, Trisk had dozed off in his seat, snoring lightly against the grain of the wooden table. A continued to wonder just how he ended up with this strange man accompanying him. He had thought the Kaligan wouldn't last a night in the outdoors given how much he complained about not staying at an inn of some kind. Yet Trisk was still there when he woke up and he had followed A without a care for his own wellbeing. A could only imagine just what had been written about him in Trisk's book. Only time would tell, he supposed.

In his lap, Clovis snuggled up to sleep as well. Curling into a ball of fluff, he yawned and closed his eyes. A shook his head at the absurdity of it all. As if Trisk's company wasn't enough, now he had a puppy following him. Well, two if he included Trisk. Then again, Trisk was more of a duckling that had imprinted on him than a puppy.

"Why do I get the feeling I'm stuck with you two" A said going back to his drink. He didn't see the need to waste it since Trisk was paying. Just as he was finished, the door to the tavern swung open and hit the wall hard with a loud thump.

Almost instantly, everyone fell silent. A looked up, tensing in his seat as two Pangarian men dressed in the uniform of the local Garrison, stele-plated armour blue fabric, came barging in followed by the old woman he and Trisk had met earlier that day.

She spotted them in the far corner "That's them!" she proclaimed with an accusing finger "Those are the thieves that stole from me!"

"Oh, you've got to be kidding me..." A whispered to himself. He tried to shake Trisk awake but he was out cold snoring away. Meanwhile, Clovis had awoken sensing his new master's unease. The pup began growling from his position on A's lap at the Garrison Officers when they reached the table.

The older of the two, forest green hair fading into moss colour with age, spoke first "Alright. Hand it over" he ordered holding out his brown gloved hand.

"Hand what over?" A asked, playing dumb.

The old woman from before barged her way forward and was nearly in his face as she screeched "My wares! You stole from my stall!" her loud nails against chalkboard voice finally rose Trisk from his drunken slumber.

"What's going on?" he groaned out.

"Mrs Ophelia claims you and your companion stole from her stall earlier this morning. Care to say anything on the matter?" the same Officer asked

Trisk blinked slowly "Yeah, she's a liar" With that, his head fell back onto the table.

The other officer, younger and newer with less patience than his partner, huffed in annoyance. "Forget him. He's too drunk to care" He focused his attention on A "As for you-" whatever he was about to say was replaced with a shrill howl of pain. Clovis had leapt off A's lap and in defence of A, had bitten into the Officer's leg and wasn't letting go.

"No, Clovis!" A gasped rising from his seat. He moved to try and pry the dog off, but the older

Officer mistook this for an act of aggression of an attempt to flee with the attention now off him. He acted without thinking, slamming the butt of his spear hard into the side of A's head. The force made A's head fling back and allowed his hood to fall back down. Suddenly, all attention in the tavern was now solely on him.

The old woman reeled back in disgust "He's a Half Breed!"

"A Half Breed?" another patron asked in shock

A hardly had time to react or even pull his hood back up when the owner Fern yelled "Get him out of here! We don't serve freaks in this place!"

Somewhere in the crowd of glaring and jeering onlookers, a single voice spoke "He's not a Freak!" but it went unnoticed. Soon enough, A found himself with his hands pinned behind his back and his face pressed into the table near Trisk. The younger Officer managed to pry Clovis off him and now held the dog by the scruff of his neck with Clovis growling and wriggling to get free.

Finally, Trisk awoke once more. This time a bit more alert than before. "What the-?"

"Little help?" asked A with a wince

Trisk took notice that A's hood was no longer up and realised how much trouble the Half breed was in. The Kaligan jumped to his feet albeit a bit unsteady and used his body weight to force the Officer from A. In doing so, he unintendedly made the Officer lose his footing and fall to the floor. The man ended up smacking his head into the wall next to the table.

"Not like that!" A yelled

"What did you expect me to do, then!?" retorted Trisk "Yell insults at him?"

Rei fumed "That's it, you sons of -!"

Their argument was swiftly brought to an end when a well-aimed punch from the younger Officer knocked Trisk clean out yet again, leaving A to face them alone. "You made a big mistake coming here, Half Breed" threatened the Officer, raising his fist to punch A as well.

"That is enough" a voice boomed from the doorway. Almost instantly, the Officer lowered his fist.

"C-Captain" stuttered the Officer, dropping Clovis as a third member of the garrison made his way towards them, the patrons of the Tavern all but jumped out of the way so he could pass. A could understand why. The captain was a Borgan. Quite an odd choice of employment for a Borgan but at this point, A didn't question it. The Officer stood to attention. "Sir, we were just dealing with-"

"Yes, I'm well aware of what you and Desmond were doing," said the captain "Honestly, the number of complaints I've received about you two, from this week along, is astounding. Now you're picking fights with travellers passing through"

The Officer stammered for a moment before pointing at A "He was causing a ruckus and he's a thief! Why else would a Half Breed be here unless it was to cause trouble?"

The Borgan Captain barely gave A a glance

before continuing his lecture "Do you have proof that he stole anything?" he spotted the old woman trying to hide herself from his gaze "Well? Did he steal from you?"

Under his imposing figure and stern gaze, she shook her head "N-no, Sir. Perhaps I was mistaken"

"What?" sneered the Officer under scrutiny "But you said – Urgh, unbelievable..."

"Just take Desmond to the sick bay. I'll sort this mess out here" That's when he spotted Trisk unconscious on the floor "Did he do this?" he asked while gesturing to the Officer. A nodded and the Borgan sighed tiredly "I do not get paid enough for this"

"Sir, if you would just let me-"

"Out. Now" he demanded not so gently, and the younger Officer knew he was serious. Shooting A one last glare, he pulled Desmond up and carried him out of the building. Clovis the opportunity to growl at him with all the might his small stature could. "Sit down," the Borgan said to A, pointing to the table where he and Trisk had been sitting before everything went wrong "I believe we need a discussion"

CHAPTER THREE

Deals & Promises

In his life, A had been in several unexpected situations. Some scary, some dangerous, some A would never like to think about again. However, this was without a doubt the strangest situation he'd been in, to date. Sitting across from him, taking three seats pushed together, sat the Borgan Captain. Urdel, he had introduced himself by. While A had a simple glass of water in his hands, Urdel drank ale straight from the barrel. His large hands easily held it up high so he could drink without issue. A was tall enough but compared to Urdel, A seemed small in comparison.

Trisk was upstairs in one of the few rooms Fern's Hall offered, sleeping off his mixture of headache and hangover with Clovis curled up beside him on the threadbare mattress. That meant Urdel was to speak to A alone. Once he was done with his barrel. Urdel had the tavern emptied so they could speak in private. A didn't like the idea but couldn't complain much in leu of his current company. Urdel soon let out a satisfied noise followed by an impressive belch from deep within his chest. He set the empty barrel down on the floor next to his feet, wiping the excess liquid off his mouth and impressive braided beard "Ahh, that hit the spot. Nothing like a good drink to finish off the day. You sure you don't want anything?"

"I'm... good. Thank you" A replied sipping at his water "Thanks for the room upstairs, by the way"

Urdel waved off his thanks "Don't worry about it. It's the least I could do for the actions of those idiotic Officers. I'll be frank. They've been on thin ice for a while now. Please. Accept my apologies for what happened"

To say A was dumbfounded was an

understatement. This was probably the first time outside of his interactions with Trisk that anyone had treated him with any form of kindness, let alone respect. The most he'd ever gotten in the past of forced civility and even that was a stretch at times. So it was safe to say A was out of his depth. "It's alright" he said weakly

"But it's not" Urdel pressed "You and your friend didn't deserve to be attacked just for it. I trained those men better than that and I expected more from them" he told him with crossed arms and a firm expression. "At any rate, you probably don't want to hear my rambling. I actually wanted to talk to you both about something important"

Fast light footsteps came down the stairs followed by slower heavier ones. Clovis appeared rounding the corner and barrelling to their table in excitement. Not far behind him was Trisk, looking exhausted and holding his head with a twisted pained expression. "I... Am never drinking again"

"Ah, just in time!" Urdel greeted loudly which

made Trisk wince even further "Please, have a seat. You're just in time" The Scan sluggishly made his way to the table and slumped onto the chair next to A. "How are you feeling, my good lad?"

Trisk removed his glasses and then covered his face with his hand "Like I drank myself stupid and got my head kicked in"

"More like punched in" A corrected in jest. Trisk's responding glare did nothing to make him feel bad. Trisk put his glasses back on and only then noticed the large Borgan sat across from them. Trisk didn't remember much but he was certain they hadn't picked up a Borgan on the way to Riven.

"Pleasure to meet you. My name is Urdel. Captain of the Riven Garrison" the much larger man greeted holding his hand out to shake his. The Scan's hand was enveloped in the bigger hand's grip. "I'll be right back. I have just the thing for that wicked headache of yours" Urdel rose from his combined seats and went over to the bar area where a solitary barmaid was cleaning up.

Trisk slowly turned his head to A "Um... What happened after I was knocked out?"

The Half Breed answered "Basically, he saved our arses. Not sure what he wants from us yet" Their newly acquired pup began pawing at his leg to be picked up. A rolled his eyes but acquiesced, bending down to pick up Clovis and place him on his lap once more. Clovis thanked him by licking at his hand till Urdel returned. He placed in front of Trisk a glass of one of a strange grey liquid that swirled and shimmered as it settled.

"Here you go. A Riven speciality. We call it Miner's delight"

"Miner's delight?" repeated Trisk questioningly

A frowned at the drink "It doesn't look very delightful"

That made Urdel chuckle "Oh trust me, it works wonders. It'll get rid of your headache faster than any healing tonic" He pushed it closer to Trisk, urging him to try it. Wanting his head to stop pounding like a mallet against his skull, Trisk gulped down the strange drink in one go. Much to the agitation of his Half Breed companion. Once the glass was empty, Trisk placed the glass back onto the table, eyes closed and silent.

A had to ask out "How was it?"

Trisk swallowed nothing "Not bad" he wheezed

"Really?"

"No" Trisk admitted gagging "It was absolutely revolting"

Urdel laughed heartedly "But it worked, did it not?" Trisk just nodded still gagging which made Urdel laugh even more "Excellent! Now, on to business!" he exclaimed with a clap of his hands. "I have something of a business venture for the two of you. Something that will be most beneficial for both of us. You see, I require help with a... delicate situation. One that really must stay out of the official records. If you catch my drift"

Suspicion rang clear between the two other men. Trisk was the first to speak. With his head no longer throbbing he could think clearly and what

Urdel was saying sounded duplicitous, to say the least. "Forgive us, but we'll need more information than that"

"Of course, of course. You see, I have a brother. The foolish thing he is has run off to join the Brotherhood of the Astrid" Urdel said with another laugh at his brother's expense "As much as I would love to leave Rylon to his prayers, I'm afraid I need him back home as soon as possible" the Borgan finished explaining

A tilted his head in confusion "Wait, you just need your brother to be returned home?" the other nodded in affirmation "Why not just get one of your officers to retrieve him?"

Urdel let out a sigh "Unfortunately, my brother was sadly something of a criminal before he left for the Brotherhood. If my superiors found out I used my officers and government funding to bring Rylon home for my own personal reasons..." he trailed off allowing them to fill in the blanks.

"Why do you need him to come home so quickly?" A questioned curiously

At that, Urdel's once boisterous expression fell into one of deep sadness "Our father is dying" he said softly "The Healers have given him till the winter. He wishes to see Rylon once more before he dies"

Trisk's pale eyes softened "Oh, I'm so sorry"

A on the other hand still had questions "Why us, though? We've only been in town a day. Why ask us at all?"

"Well, why not?" Urdel asked back as if it was the simplest thing in the world "I've always found that the ones you can trust most are the strangers who come into your life when you least expect it but need them most. I've never been wrong before about my intuition. I'm sure you two will bring my brother home. And the dog, of course" A and Trisk still looked doubtful. Noticing this, Urdel reached into his clothing and pulled out a heavy coin purse. Followed by another, then another, then another.

Soon five bags were sat on the table between them. "Five hundred gold. Yours if you bring my brother home. This," he pushed one of the bags towards them "Is your down payment. The rest you get when Rylon is by my father's sick bed"

Five hundred gold. A had never seen that much coin in his life. Living for so long off the scraps of others, he was rendered speechless for a good while. With coin like that, A doubted even the most hard-hearted of individuals would turn him away from their doorsteps. For the first time in what seemed like decades, excitement began to build within him. A's excitement dwindled when reality hit once more. Urdel's offer was too good to be true. Something was telling him that something was off about the whole thing.

A's light blue eyes narrowed "Alright, what's the catch?"

"Catch?" Urdel repeated

The Half Breed turned his attention to Trisk, whispering "He's asking two complete strangers to go pick up his criminal brother from who knows where, and he's willing to pay nearly a fortune to do so. You don't think that's odd?"

"No, I was thinking the same thing. Way too convenient" Trisk whispered back.

"Would it help if I added some kind of insurance?" offered Urdel with a kind smile regaining their attention "A way to quell any suspicions you two might have" He reached into his armour yet again and this time pulled out a rolled-up piece of parchment, sealed with the Riven blue stamp of the nearby mountain range. "This decrees that you both are under the protection of the Garrison of Riven and its sister towns. Signed by yours truly"

Even A couldn't come up with anything against that. He and Trisk shared a long silent look, both seemingly coming to the same conclusion. "Where is your brother located? Before we make any arrangements" Trisk asked.

"The last I heard; he's gone to the Monastery of

Mardern"

A baulked in surprise "What? That's halfway across the country. It'll take us weeks to get there by foot"

"Not by horse, it's not" the captain corrected. "The journey there and back will take a month at most"

It appeared Urdel had an answer for everything. "I wouldn't mind visiting Mardern again," said Trisk a bit wistfully "The rising sun on the mountains is a site to see"

"Then... I guess we have a deal" A announced with a long sigh. Urdel practically jumped with glee, slamming his hands on the table with excitement. The poor barmaid nearly dropped the glass she was cleaning out of shock. He shook their hands vigorously to the point both their chairs were bouncing in place. After a few more minutes of idle chatter, mostly Trisk noting down important details of their upcoming journey, Urdel made his goodbyes and set off. Wishing them well in their endeavour and to give Rylon his best when they did eventually meet him.

Feeling somewhat drained by the encounter with Urdel, the pair along with Clovis retreated upstairs to get some sleep before they set off tomorrow. Fern gave A a dirty look but said nothing as they ascended the stairs. The upstairs of Fern's Hall was slightly less dirty in comparison, but the scent of coal power was just as strong. So much that A gagged a little as it hit his nose. Trisk led the way to their room. Simply decorated with two beds, a single table and an oil lamp underneath the window. The beds were bare mattresses with a thin pillow and a questionably clean blanket. Hardly the lap of luxury. Without a word, A took the table and propped it under the door handle so no one could get in.

"So, what do you think? Can we trust him?" asked Trisk sitting on one of the beds.

A shrugged "I don't really trust anyone" he said taking the other bed for himself. His gaze turned to the window between the beds. Now that the sun had set, the town glowed yellow and orange with the light of oil lamps in windows. Through the smog, it was like floating lanterns drifting across a misty lake.

"I used to love this place as a kid" Trisk said stroking Clovis on his lap and looking out onto the village with a nostalgic smile "My Uncle would take me hiking all over. Said it was imperative I get back to nature" His eyes turned sad "That mine wasn't here the last time I visited"

"It wasn't?"

Trisk shook his head "No. Most of the land used to be farmland. You'd see golden wheat fields for miles on end in the summer. I think I preferred it here more than back home" Sensing his inner sadness, Clovis began nuzzling at his hand "Hey, A?" he asked, "Do you think he'd be disappointed in me?"

"Disappointed? How?"

"You know" the Scan exhaled "I wasn't here for the burial. Other than through letters, I haven't spoken to my family in years. I'm so different than what people expect of me"

`At that A rolled his eyes "Trisk, take it from someone who is definitely not what people expect. I think you're just fine" With that, he laid down on the bed which was honestly less comfortable than the forest floor they'd slept on the previous night.

Trisk smiled softly laying down as well, placing his glasses on the windowsill and Clovis curling up against him "Thanks A" After the day they had, it didn't take long for either man to fall asleep. Soon the room was filled with soft breathing and the occasional ruffs from a dreaming Clovis. Some hours later, long after the village had gone quiet and the lights dimmed, Clovis would awaken from the stuttered breaths of A.

The dog turned his head and found A tossing and turning in sleep, face scrunched up and fingers gripping the blanket in a white-knuckle grip. Yawning, Clovis hopped down off Trisk's bed and padded over to A's side of the room.

He licked at A's outstretched hand hanging off the bed which made A gasp awake. Panting, A looked to see it was only Clovis. He breathed a sigh of relief.

"Thanks" he whispered simply. He hadn't had a nightmare like that in years.

Meanwhile, Urdel returned to the barracks on the outskirts of Riven. Built of grey stone and high walls, it stood imposingly in the distance, warning anyone not to come near. As soon as he reached the doors, his façade fell away. The doors swung open and Urdel marched inside. Mere seconds later, all nearby officers and soldiers stood at attention, saluting as he passed. "Where are officers Desmond and Rei?"

"Waiting in your office, captain. As you requested" one man answered

He nodded and continued on till he reached his office door. Inside Desmond sat on one of the available chairs while Rei had a book in his hands from the office's bookshelf. Unlike the other officers, they did not stand for attention or quake in their armoured boots at the sight of him. They instead gave him a knowing nod while he locked the door behind him.

"They fell for it?" Rei inquired

Urdel smiled wickedly "Of course they did. They were sceptical at first, but I managed to convince them"

Desmond rolled his eyes "I should hope so. I took a blow to the head to make them believe it." Urdel responded to his comment by tossing a small pouch of clinking coins at him.

"For your trouble" the Borgan muttered taking a seat in his massive, custom-made purple velvet chair. The chair creaked under his weight regardless. "I can safely assume Lord Callum has been contacted?"

With a cough, Desmond nodded "Yes. Sent a raven when we returned just as you asked. You should expect a response from Lord Callum in a few days' time"

"Wonderful" Urdel mused with his hands under

his chin "Get rid of my pesky brother and a useless Half Breed all in one go. Wonders never cease" he chuckled in mirth to himself while the other men grew quiet. When Desmond and Rei had joined the Garrison, they had thought working under a Borgan would mean an easier position. Borgans were used as peacekeepers and diplomats if they ever did join up.

Urdel had successfully kept Riven and its neighbouring towns in check since his ascension to the position of Captain, but his methods had caused quite a stir among the other recruits.

Urdel began reading through the paperwork he'd left unfinished on his desk when Rei suddenly spoke up "You... You never told us why you're sending them to Mardern" Desmond's head snapped around silently gesturing for his younger colleague to stop but Rei continued "It's just – If we're getting involved in this, we deserve to know what we're getting into"

"Rei" the older Pangarian whispered in warning.

Urdel rose from his seat and made his way over to Rei. The Borgan appeared triple his size at that moment, towering over Rei with bulging crossed arms, sharp topaz eyes glaring, mouth curled, shadow looming, brow furrowed. Behind stood Desmond completely unable to move out of fear. Rei, for all his earlier courage, was frozen against the wall.

"I believe we've had this conversation before, Rei Demore," the impossibly taller man said in a mockingly gentle tone, followed swiftly by a hard punch to the gut. Rei crumpled to the floor, his armour doing nothing against the strength of the Borgan. "Know. Your. Place. Understand?"

"Y-Yes, captain" Rei managed to wheeze pathetically

"Good. Now get out of my sight. The both of you" he instructed firmly. Desmond moved to help Rei up, but Rei pushed his helping hands away, muttering that he could do it himself. Hunched over slightly, Rei left the office. Desmond followed, giving his superior a salute before doing so. Now alone, Urdel returned to his desk. Borgans were pacifists, peacekeepers, and loathed to involve themselves in fighting, that much was true. Only Urdel considered himself above all that nonsense. Above the drivel his brother preached.

When old woman Prissila came pounding on their door raving about thieves stealing from her, Urdel ordered she'd be sent away as this was quite a common occurrence for her. But then she claimed something peculiar. She had claimed one of the thieves was like no one she'd ever seen before. Tall like a Kaligan but with the skin of a Pangarian. She also swore to him that she caught sight of blue hair peeking out from under his hood. Hearing that, Urdel couldn't believe his luck. There was only one person he knew of who matched that description.

After three years since that day, Lord Callum had thought A was dead. It turns out he was mistaken. Urdel couldn't wait for his response. He didn't doubt Lord Callum would help in his endeavour. Lord Callum would get his revenge and Urdel would be rid of his brother once and for all. Rather fair if you asked him.

Lower down in the barracks, Desmond gently led Rei to his bunk. "You shouldn't have done that," he said like a father disciplining his child "You know what Captain Urdel is like"

"I know, I know" huffed Rei as he sat down on the bed "Ask a stupid question and you get a punch to the gut. Lesson learned" He slowly shifted his position to lie down properly "So what's he got planned anyway? Did he tell you?" Desmond didn't respond "Oh, you do know!"

The older hurriedly shushed him "Keep your voice down. People can hear you" He looked around at the mostly empty bunks save for a few on the far side of the room where there was nothing but heavy snoring to be heard. Desmond pinched the bridge of his nose to calm himself before speaking once more "Look, I don't know much. All I know is that Callum guy is out for the Half breed's blood. Apparently, he did something that led to the death of Callum's oldest son" the older explained, voice barely above a whisper.

Rei's eyes widened "Really? Wow, he doesn't look the part. Wait, that doesn't explain why Urdel is involved"

The door to the bunk room opened and Desmond jumped out of his skin "I've said too much already. Just go to sleep" With that, he all but fled to his own bunk ignoring Rei calling after him in a harsh whisper. He gave up once Desmond was out of earshot, lying back down on his pillow with an aggravated huff. He hated not being in the know, especially when it involved him.

He lay there in the dark with his arms at his side thinking over what he had just learned. He wondered just what he was being dragged into regarding this business with the Half Breed. It wasn't like he could simply walk away and be done with it. Urdel would never allow it. He'd never make it past Riven's gates even if he tried.

"Know your place" Rei repeated to himself. Sighing, he settled down for what would no doubt be a restless sleep.

The next morning, Trisk, A, and Clovis were up with the dawning sun. Or rather, Trisk had dragged a sleep-deprived A out of bed along with a yawning puppy. He wanted to get a head start on gathering supplies before they departed Riven later that day. A was still unsure of how wanting some new boots spanned into accepting a job to bring a wayward Borgan home. Trisk truly was affecting his life in so many odd ways and it hadn't even been three days yet. Before stepping out of the Tavern, A put his hood back up as usual. Though his identity was now known to the people of Riven, he'd rather avoid any further unpleasantries.

That morning, people gave them a wide berth both out of trepidation and fear. Something of a common occurrence for A but rather strange for Trisk. Word had spread of Urdel's interference and now the people of Riven wouldn't look them in the eye. The pair also discovered that the vendors had drastically reduced their prices for them. A was unable to find boots his size so had to make do with purchasing leather straps to hold his boots together underneath the arch and over the boot's vamp. Trisk also ended up with quite the collection of new writing supplies along with the rest of their needed items.

The butcher glared at A and Trisk but did end up throwing Clovis a Bore bone which Clovis happily held in his mouth as he toddled alongside them. When they were done gathering what they needed, their last stop was the local stable. In Riven, the horses were used within the mines pulling carts up and down the tunnels and transporting hefty loads of coal to wherever they needed to go.

The stables stank of wet hay and manure. The building looked like it could fall apart at any minute, the wood rotting away with several holes in the thatched roof. The horses themselves appeared well cared for despite their abysmal accommodations.

Trisk could at least take comfort that the animals weren't suffering. "Hello?" he called out

Out of one of the stalls stepped a Kaligan man. He wore mud-caked clothing and had some hay tangled in his wild white hair, but he had the biggest smile either of them had seen. "Good morning!" he greeted grandly "Nice to meet you both. Name's Doscal. How can I help you?"

"We were told by Captain Urdel we could rent horses from you. We can pay you for your trouble"

Doscal nodded knowingly "Aye, the Captain did send word about that. Though I have to say, renting out some of my best mares for about a month... it's going to cost you" he explained with a hand on his hip "So what are you offering? I won't go any lower than ten gold each"

Trisk let out a scoff at the price "Sir, we want to rent your horses. Not buy them off you. Ten gold each is absurd"

"From what I've heard, you can afford it" shrugged Doscal, his earlier happy exterior disappearing. Trisk and A gave each other a look before A stepped forward. He was as tall as Doscal but due to his mixed heritage, was bigger built and dwarfed the Kaligan horse master.

"I think we can come to some arrangement" A said, eyes flashing a warning "Five gold each, and we don't tell Captain Urdel that you tried to scam us" Trisk produced the letter which promised them safety to travel, signed by Urdel himself, all with a polite smile.

Doscal relented "Fine. Five gold then. But I'm charging you extra should they get hurt or you pair lose them" he warned in return then stepped back from A. "Follow me if you please. Your horses are down here" he guided them down the dirt and hay covered path between horse stalls. Clovis plopped down at the entrance, waiting for his masters to return. Small dogs and big horses did not mix after all. "For you," Doscal said to Trisk "One of my Thoroughbreds. She's fast and agile but don't push her too far too quickly. Windracer, we call her"

Windracer was a sturdy-looking mare with a dark brown coat and light brown mane. White patches on her legs and forehead popped out against her leather harness. She stepped closer to the Scan curiously, snorting in his face as a sort of greeting.

"And for you," Doscal said to A taking him to the next stall over "My Kingsbread Friesian. She'll get you where you need to go, so long as you give her apples. This we call Firefoot"

Firefoot was completely midnight black with a matching mane and tail. Her saddle and harness were the only things of colour you could see. Firefoot bobbed her head and let out a whinny, eager to get out and ride. Doscal untethered the two horses and led them back out onto the grounds. After receiving his payment of ten gold coins, he let the two men saddle up.

Trisk had ridden horses before as a child and easily got on his horse. A, not so much. Thankfully, Firefoot was of a calm disposition and waited in place till A was securely on her. Clovis was placed into Trisk's satchel which he moved to rest in between his legs. The pup's head poking out of the flap.

"Where are we headed first?" Questioned A, grasping the reigns in a white-knuckle grip.

Trisk pulled out the map from his coat pocket "Let's see... Ah. We need to follow that road," he pointed ahead of him "Then take a left turn at the next fork in the road"

"I better see you two back here in a month, you hear me?" warned Doscal "Right, off you go" he smacked Firefoot's rear, giving her the signal to run. Only Firefoot didn't run. She bolted. With A shouting in fright as she did. Trisk kicked his horse and chased after the Half Breed.

"How do you stop this thing!?" A cried, voice fading the further away he got.

"Hang on A!" Trisk yelled stifling his laughter. All the while Doscal chuckled, tossing the coins in his hands with satisfaction.

CHAPTER FOUR

New Companion

On the way to Riven, along the dirt path with transfer papers in hand, walked Yuen. He wore his simplest clothing so as to not draw suspicion to himself, long black hair half braided up to reveal his rounded ears. In truth, Yuen was a well-known and sought-after member of the Royal Guard.

He'd joined up at the tender age of sixteen and never looked back. He did have an odd habit of transferring to different outposts every few months, but his pristine record left little room for others to ask any unwanted questions. On his person was an over-the-shoulder leather satchel that contained his personal effects and several important pieces of paper that he never travelled anywhere without.

Yuen took a long breath, taking in the last bit of fresh air before he hit the smoggy village of Riven. He had been warned in advance that the village would be far from picturesque with the pollution from the local mines. He had to admit, the warning had been correct. Even in the distance, he could see just how blackened and filthy the small village was in stark contrast to the rest of the surrounding area.

He looked to his left for a moment to take in the lush green hills that had patches of wildflowers dotted here and there. He could hear hoof beats against the road but thought little of it, till he turned to look ahead once more, and he saw a horse galloping straight towards him with its light blue-haired rider barely hanging on. Yuen darted out of the way just in time, feeling the wind race by as the horse shot past him. He had landed on the grass feeling a little bewildered at what he had just seen.

Moments later, before Yuen had even gotten his bearings back, a second rider came galloping past him at equal speeds. Yuen clambered back to his feet wiping off the dirt off his clothing, silently wondering what the rush was about. With a shake of his head, Yuen promptly forgot about the strange encounter and continued to the mining village. He had an appointment to keep after all. While Riven had its main gates, he had come in the opposite direction which led him through the less populated area that connected to the marketplace "Excuse me?" he asked a passing villager "Can you point me to the barracks?"

The villager, an elderly gentleman of long silver hair and pointed ears, grunted and pointed with his walking stick to the lone grey stone building that was about a ten-minute walk from where Yuen stood. "Thank you," the Pangarian said with a nod "Oh. Does this village have a notice board?"

Yuen was told in less than friendly words, that the notice board was located in the marketplace next to the fountain. Yuen found the weathered wooden notice board littered with scraps of paper telling of what stalls were open, what deals were going on, and much to Yuen's puzzlement, several badly written poems.

He pulled out one of the papers from his satchel, pausing to look at it with a heavy heart. Yuen pinned the paper up and then walked away. The paper he had left behind flapped lightly in the breeze. On it read a simple message.

Yuin, please come home.

Yuen arrived at the barracks and when introducing himself, was hastily ushered into Captain Urdel's Office. He wasn't even given time to change into his new uniform when the door to the office was slammed shut on him, leaving him to wait for his new Captain with uncertainty. He had been told that Riven's Captain was a Borgan before he left his previous outpost. Yuen had gotten along well with other Borgans and didn't think it would be any different this time.

"Ah, Guard Delson" Urdel greeted entering the office

"Please, call me Yuen. Guard Delson sounds like

my father" Yuen joked to break the ice. It seemed to work as Urdel let out a chuckle.

"Very good. Very good. Do you have your transfer papers?" in response Yuen fished the envelope out of his satchel and handed it to the Borgan. Urdel sat on his massive chair which only enunciated just how much bigger he was compared to Yuen, and Yuen was no small Pangarian himself. The Borgan glanced at the papers humming thoughtfully. "You have a pristine record. Several commendations for bravery and valour from your superiors. Though I notice you've never stayed in one place longer than a few months. Why is that?"

Yuen sat up in his chair, back straight as an arrow "I go wherever I'm needed, Sir. If that means I'm constantly on the go, then that's what I'll need to do" That was the story Yuen used whenever asked why he kept on the move and not settle in one post. The real reason he kept close to his heart.

"I understand. I'm not fond of staying in one spot for too long either" Urdel handed back the papers "In fact..." he smiled "I believe I may have a job for you"

※ ※ ※

"Well, that was certainly something" Trisk commented well after catching up to A and his wayward horse. Riven was some miles behind them by then, the sun now high in the sky with barely a cloud to be seen. Trisk was glad to be able to smell something other than soot and coal. He had Firefoot tethered to Windracer by the reigns trotting at a much slower pace. A sat silently on the saddle holding a whimpering Clovis who had not enjoyed the chase on horseback in the slightest. "Oh, come on. It wasn't that bad"

A only gave him an unamused glare. Trisk would swear that even the dog was side-eyeing him. For once A had his hood down, not bothering to pull it back up after nearly being thrown off his horse. He was still rather baffled as to how he'd gotten roped up into this.

How he had allowed what was essentially a total stranger into his isolated life and shake its foundations. A was alone and that's all he'd ever be. He'd accepted that as fact many years ago. So why did Trisk, a Scan from the North who probably should have stayed in his Library for his own safety, end up being someone A didn't have to avoid?

Questions like that filled his thoughts till Trisk brought the horses to a stop by a river for them to drink. A was just glad to get his feet on solid ground. He held no ill will to Firefoot as she was only doing what horses do, but he was not looking forward to getting back on.

Clovis leapt from his arms and began running in circles till he found a good spot to do his business. A recognised the area. He also realised that if they crossed the shallow river, they'd find Lamb Grove pass which would shave at least a week off their journey. It was a little-known shortcut that would take them indirectly to Elayas. The last stop on the map before they reached Mardern.

"You know, if we go in this direction, we'll find a shortcut that will get us there sooner"

"Really?" Trisk asked, glancing up and down to his map in confusion "I don't know. I think we should stick to the map"

A rolled his eyes "Trisk, I've used this path myself before. I'm telling you; we'll be in Elayas by the end of the week if you go this route" Trisk still appeared apprehensive. A sighed "Fine, we'll stick to the main road if it makes you feel better"

"Very much so" Trisk answered smiling. They stayed at the riverbank till the horses had their fill of water and had rested a little. "Alright. Now let's... Um, A? Where's Clovis?" the Scan asked, realising the ball of fluff that had been latched onto them was nowhere in sight. Both men looked around the area but saw no sign of him other than the dog mess he had left behind. "I thought you were watching him"

"Me? You're the one that insisted we take him with us" retorted A

"Well, you named him!"

"You fed him!"

Their argument was cut short when they recognised Clovis's bark coming from within the treeline that covered one side of the lake. The puppy must have slipped away when neither was looking. When the barks turned to growls, Trisk burst into a run following the noise "Hang on, Clovis! I'm coming!"

"Wait!" A yelled "You can't just run blindly into the – and he's gone" The Half-Breed let out a sigh of frustration. A debated on what he should do next but realised he had to follow. Muttering some rather choice words under his breath, A tied up the horses to a tree so they wouldn't also run off, then went to find Trisk. "I didn't even want the damn dog..." he complained marching after the wayward Scan and lost puppy. "Trisk! Wait up!"

Running further into the trees, Trisk chased after the sounds of Clovis. He could only hope he was heading in the right direction and not running around in circles. He'd done that before and would like to avoid such embarrassment. "Clovis? Where are you, boy?" he called out. He heard further growling and barking and headed in that direction. Or what he could discern was that direction. "Clovis?"

"Trisk?" A's voice echoed from behind him

Trisk was relieved to hear a familiar voice "Over here! I think he went this way. Clovis!"

The Half Breed trudged his way towards him through winding exposed tree roots and small gaps between the trees. The further in the got, the thicker the forest seemed to become. "He's not going to answer you. It's a dog, not one of those weird talking birds from the Capital"

Trisk shuddered "Ergh, don't remind me. One of those things once followed squawking insults all day. Clovis!" he tried once more, this time cupping his hands around his mouth to further his voice. There was a resounding growl that followed, far deeper and louder than Clovis could muster. Trisk took a step forward and then promptly disappeared from A's line of sight.

"Trisk?" A asked in shock. He too took a few steps forward and, like Trisk, did not see the hole that had been hidden in the forest floor.

Not too far away, Yuen stood there with a rather flummoxed expression.

A landed with a splash which was unexpected when falling down a hole in the forest. He spluttered for breath when his head surfaced, every part of him soaked through. He saw Trisk standing knee-high in the water, just as wet as he was. As it turned out, they had both slipped into a tunnel that was connected to a deep well. Above them was a hole that allowed enough light in to see clearly.

"What happened?" asked Trisk

"We're both in a well. That's the extent of my knowledge" A stated sarcastically. It was only then did the powerful smell of what they were standing in hit him. He twisted up his nose in confusion. "Is..." he looked down at what they were standing in "Are these berries?"

Upon closer inspection, he realised they were knee-deep in berries of every colour and variation soaking in a purple sugary mixture that made A's teeth ache just from the small taste he'd had.

"Oh, thank goodness it wasn't just me" sighed Trisk "Yeah, I'm confused too. Why is there a pit of berries in the middle of a forest?" They would soon get their answer when more berries, red in colour, were dumped into the well from above, bouncing onto A's already sopping hair.

"Hey, watch it!" he yelled up to whoever was up there. The head of a small child appeared over the rim of the topside of the well. Bright purple eyes looked down on them curiously.

"Hey! Hey, get us out of here!" Trisk all but begged the child. The child nodded, seeming a little shocked, then disappeared. Hopefully to find help. "Wait, why is a child out in the middle of the forest?" he asked A baffled

A simply shrugged "I'm more curious as to the whole berry thing going on here" he looked down and groaned, lifting one foot out of the mixture "And my boots are officially ruined. Just what I needed"

"Are you alright?" Trisk asked with a frown when he noticed A's breathing was quickening and the Half Breed's face had gone a remarkable shade of pale.

"I'm fine" A snapped swallowing "I just... don't like closed spaces"

Miraculously, a rope was thrown down from above. The child had returned much to their combined relief. Trisk went first being the lighter of the two. Though with wet hands and not that much upper body strength, getting out was going to be a challenge.

"Ok, you lot. What are you doing now?" a female voice asked from above

"We're trying to get the funny men out of the hole" a child explained

The woman laughed "Trying to get the funny men out of the hole. I must admit, that's a new one" Her head came into view peering down, not expecting the children to be correct. Imagine her surprise when she saw they were telling the truth "Oh, by the Four" she gasped "Hang on! We'll get you out!"

"Thank you!" Trisk responded, holding on as best he could as he was hoisted up. Then it was A's turn. It took a little longer to pull him up compared to Trisk, but he was just glad to be out. The woman who helped them out was a young Pangarian woman, with short sunshine-yellow hair and sunset-gold eyes. She wore a simple muted brown dress with a white blouse underneath.

The pair realised the well they had ended up in was in the centre of a campsite. Dozens of tents and wooden caravans on wheels were dotted around several small campfires. Washing lines filled with drying clothing and multi-coloured banners hung from almost every available branch.

There were also massive vats of berries scattered around, sorted into colours and ready to be pressed. Bundling towards them, a familiar ball of fluff yapped for their attention. "Clovis!" Trisk exclaimed kneeling to catch the dog. Clovis ignored him entirely and instead pawed at A's ruined boot-covered feet, whining to be picked up.

The Pangarian woman smiled and giggled slightly "Oh, he's yours. I wondered where this little fellow came from" she said as A eventually picked him up "My name is Mari. Come on, you can dry off at my place" she gestured for them to follow

The Scan suddenly gasped "Wait. Oh no! A, our horses! They've probably bolted by now"

"Don't worry. I tied them up before I went after you. They should still be by the river" A explained whilst trying to avoid getting his nose nipped once more.

"The river? Oh, that's no problem. I'll have someone fetch them here for you" Mari then gestured for them to follow her. "Come on. You guys can dry off at my place. And bring the puppy"

Starting to feel cold in their wet clothing, the

two men plus Clovis followed her through the campsite. Mari seemed nice enough, her gold eyes kinder than most A had seen in his lifetime which made him just a smidge less hesitant to follow her. Mari's caravan was located under shady trees with colourful glass charms swaying gently in the breeze. The caravan itself was painted a light purple with blue window frames. Smoke puffed out of the metal pipe on the roof.

"Col? Can you fetch these men's horses? They should be by the river" she called out to the man sitting on a tree stump smoking a pipe. The pointed-eared Kaligan nodded and went off to fetch the horses Trisk and A had left behind. A paused for a second, doing a double take as he could have sworn he'd seen that man before. His thoughts were interrupted when Trisk all but shoved him into Mari's caravan.

They were hit instantly with warmth from the small wood-burning stove and the aroma of dried herbs. The inside was larger than it had appeared from the outside. They had entered through the door and into a small sitting area that was connected to the small cooking area. Further down were three doors that led to the rest of the interior. Every inch of available space was littered with clutter of all kinds. Stacks upon stacks of books. Trinkets that sparkled and shimmered in the firelight. Hanging bottles and decorations made it nigh impossible to move without bumping your head into something. Lit and unlit candles. "I'll fetch some towels for you. You can hang your wet clothes on the rack there" Mari turned to walk away "Oh. And watch out for Theo. He's around here somewhere"

"Theo?" questioned A

"You're not the only one with a dog around these parts. He's small but he's a feisty little thing. Belongs to my friend Rosilyn" She left them to get sorted. A set Clovis down on one of the plump pillows that laid on the floor near the stove. Like Trisk, he slowly began removing their wet and berry-smelling clothes when Trisk paused suddenly, unconsciously smiling at something A couldn't see. "What is it?"

"I've just realised. You've had your hood down this entire time, and she hasn't commented once" he whispered. A hadn't even realised that had happened. His hand reached up to find that Trisk was correct. A's Half-Breed nature had been on show the entire time and Mari hadn't said a word. In fact, now that he thought of it, many people in camp must have seen him unhooded and no one seemed to even bat an eyelid.

A had to take a seat on one of the armchairs feeling rather rattled at the development. Trisk took pity and took his wet cloak and hung it on the rack next to the stove along with his cloak and jacket. Mari then returned with two large towels, warm and fluffy in different shades of green.

"Here you go. Sorry about the whole ending up in the berry pit. I've been saying we need to get that hole filled in for months now" she sighed giving them the towels "Seriously. Someday, that hole is going to kill somebody"

"Um... If you don't mind me asking" Trisk inquired "But what's up with all the berries?"

Mari let out an annoyed heavy sigh, plopping herself on the sofa "You can blame Pinches for that"

It was A's turn to look confused "I'm sorry, Pinches?"

"He's our resident Oracle. Or he claims to be. He lives in the last caravan down there. The big gaudy one decked out in gemstones" she said, gesturing with her thumb "He's got most people around here convinced that he can 'tell the future' or 'grant your wishes' or my favourite 'speak to the spirits'. That kind of rubbish" Mari was clearly not impressed recounting what she knew. "He claims that if you donate berries in his name, whatever you want will be given to you" She rolled her eyes "Hence, the pit. That's where the reject berries go"

"Well, doesn't he sound... interesting" remarked the Scan, his hair tinged a slight purple from ending up in said pit.

"Word of advice? Don't listen to a word that idiot says" She stood up once more "Let me see if I have any spare clothes around here. I'm sure Rosilyn keeps some in her trunk..."

When Mari had left for a second time, A turned to Trisk looking flummoxed "She still didn't say anything!" he said whispering harshly "I don't get it"

Trisk shrugged "Maybe she doesn't care? I mean, I don't"

A shot him a look "Trisk, the first day we met, you wanted an interview with a 'one of a kind' as you put it"

"Oh... yeah, I was hoping you had forgotten about that"

"Ah ha!" Mari announced from one of the bedrooms "I knew she had some around here somewhere" the woman returned, this time with her arms filled with clothing. "This should do till your clothes dry out. I'll leave you to – oh there you are" she announced kneeling. When she stood back up, she had a dog even smaller than Clovis in her arms. Theo was a tiny thing of short black and tan fur with tufts of thicker fur at the muzzle. Theo was also incredibly hyper, wriggling in Mari's arms and panting madly, licking any part of her face he could get at.

The door to the caravan opened "Mari? Are you home? I heard we have visitors" said a sweet-sounding woman. In entered another Pangarian woman with thick black hair tight up into a messy bun, glowing amber skin and red painted lips that surrounded a mischievous smile. Her teeth resembled rows of shining pearls and she was decked out in glamourous multi-coloured fabrics that made up her outfit created out of bright and glossy silks and tulle. She took one look at the scene, of Mari with two somewhat dressed me, and laughed "Oh my" she said fanning herself "Shall I come back later?"

"No!" all three gasped in unison, only then realising just how it looked. Trisk and A hurriedly dressed in the offered clothing.

"I heard someone had fallen into Pinches pit. I take it, it was these strapping young men?"

"That's them. This is…"

Trisk answered for her "I'm Trisk. Scan of the Redencon Library and this is my friend, A" he motioned to A who waved at the two women a little anxiously at the attention now being on him.

Rosilyn "Oh my goodness. Dear, when was the last time you ate?" she questioned A, not commenting on his appearance or heritage in the slightest "Mari, get a pot going. Our guests must be starving!" the older woman brushed past them and headed to help Mari.

A averted his eyes back to Trisk, resembling that of a lost kitten "Now I'm just confused"

❃ ❃ ❃

Rosilyn insisted the pair stay the night in their caravan, ignoring any objections the two men had. After being fed enough hearty vegetable stew to feed at least three grown men, Trisk and A were given pillows and blankets and told to make themselves comfortable in the sitting area. The blankets had been woven by Rosilyn herself, her perfected craft after years of practice. She would sell them at markets for a good price and use the money to help the others in her campsite.

After making sure the horses were secure and bringing their bags inside, Trisk and A were both sound asleep with Clovis curled up on A's rising and falling chest.

"What a peculiar pair they make" Rosilyn observed handing Mari a steaming cup of herb tea "Did you find out where they're headed?"

Mari took a sip before answering "Apparently, they're heading to Marden. Some job they need to complete, I think"

It went quiet for a while. Each woman silently drank their tea while thinking. Rosilyn voiced without warning "Why don't you go with them"

Mari choked on her tea "W-What?"

"I said, why don't you go with them?" the older woman pressed "Come now dearie, you don't want to live here the rest of your life"

Mari shook her head "I like it here. Even with Pinches setting up shop"

"But are you happy here?" asked the black-haired woman softly. Mari's face fell at the question "Listen, darling, I know you're worried about what might happen if you leave here. But it's been ten years. I think you're safe by now"

"... How can you be sure?"

"I'm not. And neither will you be. But you can't live your life living in fear. Or else one day you'll be my age and regret never taking that leap into the unknown" Mari was about to speak but Rosilyn cut her off "Just think about it, will you? Don't let those people control you still. Not when you fought so hard to free yourself"

Mari craned her neck to look at the sleeping pair "Do you think I can trust them?"

"Well, you trusted me, and you didn't know

me either. And besides, should anything happen, I'm sure I've taught you well enough to fend for yourself" she winked, and Mari stifled a laugh remembering the kind of teaching Rosilyn had given her.

The next morning, a third horse was waiting next to Firefoot and Windracer. Named Highclere, the Meridian Warmblood was a strongly built horse with a greyish-white coat and black mane and tail. Trisk and A had been taken aback when it was announced Mari would be going with them. The young woman had changed out of her dress and into breaches, boots, a red blouse with a black waistcoat, and a cloak gifted from Rosilyn. Along with a brown sack of personal effects, Mari had with her a small hardback book. Something she never went anywhere without.

"Oh! I almost forgot. These are for you" Mari announced, producing from behind her back a pair of black leather, knee-length boots. A took the offered boots in disbelief. He had no idea where she had gotten them, but he wasn't complaining in the slightest. He turned to Trisk "She's coming"

"What!?" Trisk asked, "Just like that?"

"I told you, I needed new boots" was all A said on the matter. Trisk wasn't that upset about it. In fact, he was pleased to have another person on the road with them. At the very least he'd have someone to talk to. A wasn't exactly the chatty sort while travelling.

Rosilyn hugged Mari tight, arms enveloping her in a tight hug. Almost everyone in the hidden community had come to say goodbye to Mari. Young and old, they all came to see her off and wish her well "You be safe now, you hear? And remember. You'll always be welcome here"

Mari nodded "I know. Thank you, Rosilyn. For everything"

"Knock them dead, dearie"

Soon enough, all three plus Clovis were setting off with Mari leading the way out of the forest and back to the road. When out of earshot, the camp was rocked with a bellowing indignant shout from the one and only Pinches "Which one of you stole my bloody boots!?"

CHAPTER FIVE

Bandits in the Forest

The campsite was a day behind them. The first night the three spent together was uneventful. They camped under the stars and feasted on the smoked fish and bread loaves Rosilyn had packed for Mari. Like before with A, Trisk didn't ask any personal questions that night for fear of offending her. Though with Trisk being Trisk, his curiosity won out the next day

"So..." Trisk finally asked a few miles down the road "What made you decide to come with us, anyway?"

Mari shrugged "Not sure. I was up all night debating whether I should leave or not. In the end, I guess... I just wanted to see what else is out there"

She smiled at the two men "Don't get me wrong, Rosilyn has been good to me. But I couldn't keep relying on her charity forever"

That caught A's attention "Charity?"

"Yeah. She found me and took me in after..." she trailed off suddenly uncomfortable "Well, I just hope I'll be able to repay her kindness one day. So, tell me about this job you have in Mardern. I'm curious"

As Trisk explained the reason why they were heading to the northern tips of the continent, A silently observed the woman who had joined them. He was still on edge despite her seemingly not caring about what he looked like in the slightest. A was unaccustomed to this.

Truthfully, he was completely out of his depth. Acceptance had never and would never be something he would know. Even Trisk had been more interested at the start of his research than in A as a person. As for Mari, well, A wasn't sure what to think. He's never met anyone who simply didn't care. The most A ever got was pure indifference.

Mari on the other hand, treated A like she would Trisk. With respect and decency which left A feeling more confused than ever if he considered the long-standing hatred between the two races.

"I don't get it" A mumbled which caught the other two off guard

"I'm sorry?" asked Mari looking back at him. Lost in thought, A had allowed Firefoot to fall behind a tad. The three horses were brought to a stop.

"I said, I don't get it" he repeated himself sounding firmer than before "Why haven't you said anything?"

Mari frowned genuinely confused "About what?"

With a huff, A pulled down his hood to show his semi-pointed ears and light blue hair. The movement jostled Clovis awake who had been peacefully snuggled up in A's Jacket since they had left "I mean this" he pointed to himself "Why haven't you said a word about this?"

Mari glanced between him and Trisk, her confusion turning to something akin to sadness "Was... was I supposed to?'

"Yes! Everyone does" explained A pulling his hood back up "Even Trisk did when we first met"

"I said I was sorry!" Trisk exclaimed with a pout

Mari cut the Half Breed off before the argument stemmed into a shouting match "Hang on. You expected me to dislike you? Solely because of who you are?" she asked, and A nodded, as if it was obvious "Wow... you've not met many nice people then, have you?" she continued with a soft smile that confused A even further. "Look, I don't care. I honestly don't. I mean, if I did care about something like that, by that logic I would also dislike Trisk just for being a Kaligan"

"Exactly" added Trisk but quickly went quiet under A's unamused glance

"So, that's it? You just don't care that I'm a Half Breed?"

She shook her head "Nope. Not at all. I'd say I

respect you"

Now A was simply dumbfounded. Even Trisk seemed puzzled at the statement "You - you respect me?"

Mari grinned "Of course I do," she said with pride in her sweet voice "I can only imagine what life must have been like for you. But look at you. You're alive. You're surviving no matter what the world throws at you. And that gets my respect" she finished with a pointed finger jabbing at his chest and a chuckle "Oh, that reminds me. I never got your name yesterday. What is it?"

The two men fell silent for a long time, so much so that Mari grew worried "Did I say something wrong?"

Trisk coughed awkwardly "Um... My friend here was never given one. He goes by A. Like the letter" he explained not looking in A's direction.

A kicked his horse into gear and took the lead "Come on, we're losing daylight" he muttered subdued. Trisk gave Mari an apologetic look and followed A's lead. The lone woman of the group kept her horse still for a moment longer, absorbing what she had heard "He doesn't have a name?" she whispered to herself so quietly the others wouldn't hear. To say she was shocked would be an understatement. She had just assumed she hadn't been informed of his name the previous day or had simply not heard it. But to know he didn't have a name of his own? Something inside Mari broke for the Half Breed. All her life, she had cared not for the animosity or hatred that seemed to plague her world. But for A, he had borne the brunt from each opposing side from the day he was born. Not even given a name to call his own.

Shaking herself out of her thoughts, Mari kicked her horse to hurry after them. She made it so she was beside A as their horses trotted along. For a while, she remained silent. Not quite sure whether her words would make things better or worse between them. Eventually, Mari spoke "Mari isn't my name"

"What?" A questioned

"Mari. It's not my name. Not my real name at least" she clarified "I changed it after I left home"

A frowned "Why are you telling me this?"

"What I'm saying, is that you could give yourself one. If you wanted to" A turned to look ahead, face steeling into an emotionless mask. He made his horse go at a faster pace not giving Mari an answer. Mari groaned as Trisk came up beside her. "I just made things worse, haven't I?"

Trisk patted her back in sympathy "It's alright. Your heart was in the right place. Your head, not so much"

She gaped at him, genuinely offended at what he said. "Well, excuse me for helping" she announced sarcastically "How's that research going if I may ask?"

Trisk flushed a vibrant shade of pink "Yes, yes, I get it" he huffed, their conversation ending there and then. Ahead of them, A's hood covered the small half-smile on his face. The first one in what was a very long time. The pup in his jacket sensed the shift in emotions and wagged his tail as best he could from inside the jacket.

Following behind at a distance on his own horse but going through the trees to avoid detection, Yuen had overheard the entirety of the conversation. His frown was deep set and brows furrowed. Just why had Urdel ordered he follow this small group on their way to Mardern? And why was he suddenly unsure of himself?

Following orders was exactly what Guardsmen do. Ask no questions. Do as commanded. Submit blindly to the will of their leader. But listening in on the three converse, and learn their stories, Yuen couldn't help but feel something was amiss with his orders from Captain Urdel. Still, he continued to follow. He had his orders, after all.

❈ ❈ ❈

The trio continued onward. The sounds of nature surrounded them, from bird songs to the rustling of leaves in the breeze. Adding to the surroundings was Mari humming as they travelled. She had been humming at random intervals the whole day but was now humming a tune neither man recognised. Her voice was pleasant to the ear and Trisk could tell she must have had some training in the past. Her humming was a welcome distraction to the quiet that had befallen them. A hadn't said a word to either of them since their earlier talk had taken an unexpected turn, and neither was keen on poking the proverbial bear just in case. Trisk found himself closing his eyes and allowing the humming to drown out his thoughts. Even while on horseback, Trisk felt he could easily drift off to sleep.

"You have a lovely voice" Trisk remarked

"Oh, thank you" replied Mari smiling "I wasn't aware I was that loud"

"No, I'm serious" the Scan insisted "Where were you trained?"

Out of the blue, A brought Firefoot to a halt

which made Mari and Trisk do the same. The Half Breed raised his hand as a signal for them to remain quiet. His pale blue eyes fixated intently on the path before them. His head tilted to the side as he focused, mouth curled down in an almost grimace.

"A? What's-"

"Shush" ordered A, hand gesturing once more at Trisk to remain silent. It was clear something had caught his attention, something neither the Pangarian nor Kaligan could see for themselves. Till they heard a rustling come from a thorn bush up ahead. Travelling through the forest would have its downsides. One of them being the unpredictable wildlife.

It was only surprising they hadn't had any interactions with the local wildlife until now. The three braced themselves for whatever was to pop out at them, be it beast or otherwise. Their shoulders untensed when only a small brown and tan coat ferret slipped out onto the path. Little paws rubbed at its face and nose twitching in the air. Mari awed aloud at the cute-looking animal.

The ferret let out a shriek when an arrow pinned it to the ground.

"Shit!" A cried, his horse bucking upwards just as loud yelling could be heard advancing on them. Mari braved a look back and saw no less than five muscular men wielding swords and bows charging at them.

"Bandits!" she screamed. Their horses began to bolt single file down the path. The next town was only a few hundred feet away, so the trio only had to outrun them long enough and they would be safe. That is if they could avoid the arrows raining down upon them. The bandits were fast on their feet, made so by the illegal elixirs they consumed on a near-daily basis.

This part of the continent had quite the problem with black market potions and bandit groups capitalized on the availability of them to ensure their targets never escaped. It made them faster, stronger, and smarter, but the potions came at a price. One that their victims would pay.

Trisk howled in pain when an arrow lodged in his upper arm through his jacket. The shock caused him to lose grip of the reigns and topple off his horse, landing hard upon the ground. Windracer continued to gallop not stopping at all. "Trisk!" Mari yelled forcing her horse to halt to try and help. That's when more bandits materialised and grabbed her, pulling her off her Highclere with great force. Said horse bolted before anyone could catch him.

A and Firefoot were nowhere in sight. Mari was forced to the ground next to the injured Trisk. Several men pinned them down with rough calloused hands. Trisk couldn't even cry out in pain due to his face practically being smashed into the dirt. His spectacles almost bent out of shape.

"Let us go!" Mari demanded as hard as she could muster. The bandits paid her no heed. They did, however, take great interest in the coin purse attached to Trisk's belt. It was snatched off the Scan before Trisk had time to realise what they wanted.

Seeing no option and deciding their lives were more important than coin, Trisk spoke "Look, just – just take it. It's all yours, just let us go!"

The main bandit, a hulking Pangarian of tattooed skin and dark mahogany hair simply laughed at their expense. The heavy coin purse was held aloft in his large hand. "We're eating good tonight, lads!" he exclaimed, followed by a rousing cheer. He tossed the purse to one of his men and smirked "Gents, have your fun"

"Oh shit" whispered Trisk

Thankfully, help arrived in the most curious of fashions. Clovis's paws pounded the dirt as he surged towards them. The pup jumped upon one of the bandits and latched his teeth onto the rounded ear. Said bandit cried out as Clovis refused to let go no matter how hard the man pulled at the wriggling puppy.

Then, galloping hoofbeats could be heard charging towards the group. A had returned with a long spear in hand, the tip sharp as an arrowhead.

In the commotion, Trisk used his good arm to grab Mari and roll them out of the path of the midnight mare. The pair ended up in the foliage that edged the sides of the path. Bandits of all shapes and sizes dove out of the way or attempted to slash at the horse with their blades. One bandit, the man who had taken the coin purse, did not manage to get out of the way in time. His dark brown eyes widened exponentially as he was thrown off his feet by the mare. The next thing the man knew was pain. Searing, heart-stopping pain radiating from his chest.

He slowly looked down only to see nothing but red. The spear pierced straight through his chest and through his back, embedding him in the large oak tree behind him. The unknown bandit struggled to lift his gaze. When he finally managed to, he saw a sight unlike no other.

A grasped the spear, a panicked expression on his face, light blue hair glowing in the sunlight. His semi-pointed ears were clear as day for anyone to see. "Wha - Half Breed...?" was all he could mumble before he went limp. As for the rest of the bandit group, they remained frozen in place, almost in a trance from what they had just witnessed.

A's head snapped towards them, now forcing a vicious expression on his face. Teeth bared and nostrils flaring. "Go" he snarled at the lot of them. The would-be thieves didn't hesitate to flee back into the forest from whence they came. Down one leader and one having lost an ear to Clovis. Said puppy padded towards them, ear still in his mouth and tail wagging at his success. A dismounted his horse, legs shaking as he took a moment to realise what he had just done and went to help his fallen comrades up to their feet. "Are you two alright?" he asked them both. His response was a bone-crushing hug from Mari who was near tears.

"Mari, he hates touch" warned Trisk. Mari had enough sense left to let go when she heard him say that.

"By the Four!" Mari gasped "Since when did

bandits get this close to towns?"

Trisk could only shrug "No idea. And by the way, for future reference, we are staying away from the forests from now on" he declared clutching his injured arm. The arrow was still in his limb but thankfully the bleeding looked minimal. "Where did you even get that spear?" he asked A, pointing to the now-dead bandit leader.

A explained "The horse bolted towards the town. I couldn't find anyone at the gates, so I took one of their weapons" he glanced over to the man he had just bested, looking a little green around the gills. "Though that was not my intention"

Trisk let out a sigh "Well, we survived but they got the coin Urdel had given us" he looked to the path the horses had gone down "And there go our supplies. Great..."

"Well, one horse is better than nothing" commented Mari trying to be helpful. "Plus, the little guy got a good bite in. Didn't you, boy? Oh, yes you did!" she cooed at Clovis, happily ignoring the severed appendage in his panting mouth.

"We should get going. You need to get that arm seen too, and I'd rather not stick around in case they come back" A took the reins of Firefoot and led the horse towards the nearby town. The town was simply called TeraKyla. Somewhere so small it was found on barely any map. The town had one street, only a few dozen houses, and one small building to house the garrison soldiers. All twelve of them. The houses themselves were relatively nice if having seen better days, built with proper bricks and colourful paint, a stark contrast to Riven and its coal dust-encrusted crumbling buildings. They could see a stall dotted here and there but most of the businesses were found in actual shops with signs hanging on the outside of their doors. There was a high, makeshift wooden fence surrounding the town but given that much of it was either burnt down or broken, it wasn't doing a very good job of keeping the town safe. Before they could enter, they were stopped by a man of the garrison. This one was decked in dull grey armour that was dented and misshapen and tattered red fabric.

"We don't allow thieves in these parts. You stole equipment belonging to the TeraKyla garrison. What do you have to say for yourselves?"

A had his hood back up by then so he was able to avoid problems concerning that. He answered "I apologise but I was sort of strapped for time. We were attacked by bandits and they -"

"Wait, bandits?" the guard asked looking shocked from what they could see of his face. He glanced past them "And you survived?!"

"You can look for yourselves if you want. Our friend here killed one of them for you" Trisk said praising A to the guard.

The guard appeared to be unable to comprehend what he was hearing. "This - this bandit. What did he look like?"

Mari answered "Um, big fellow? Reddish hair, lots of tattoos"

Now he was open-mouthed, gaping at them in

utter incredulousness. Then, he ran back into the town yelling at the top of his lungs. "He's dead! Atdroc is dead!"

"Who?" Trisk asked with confusion

"I believe it might be the man I killed" A answered with a disquiet look on his face. Out of nowhere, people were coming out of their houses in droves, all whispering or muttering the same thing. That Atdroc was dead. When they caught sight of the three people at the entrance of their humble town, their cheers could be heard for miles. For the trio, they were just woefully confused as to what was going on. Pangarians, Kaligans, Borgans, and people of all kinds rushed to them, praising them and thanking them profusely. Some of the oldest town folk, those who could barely stand upright due to their age, practically kissed their boots in gratitude.

"Everyone!" cried the guard that had sounded the call for attention "No longer shall we live in fear. For today, Atdroc has met his creator. Our heroes of

TeraKyla have at last arrived!" another rousing cheer exploded from the gathered crowd.

Trisk leaned over to A and said "Congrats. You're a hero"

The Half Breed just grunted in response, holding his hood tight so it wasn't tugged off by wandering hands. Back on the path, Yuen inspected the body of Atdroc and whistled to himself. He was both impressed and somewhat unnerved. He's recognised the dead man from having dealings with him in the past. Atdroc was or had been, an incredibly dangerous and unpredictable bandit. Even more so when under the influence of black-market elixirs. He'd vanished some months ago and most had assumed or rather hoped he was gone for good. It turns out he was just in hiding, using the nearby town as his personal hunting ground.

Now the infamous Atdroc was dead, and his killer was a Half Breed. Yuen was impressed that a simple Half Breed was capable of such action. From what he had seen, the one known as A mostly stayed out of trouble when he could.

Yet here he had acted without thinking twice, taking down a ruthless bandit leader and saving his comrades. Yuen jotted down his findings and whistled once more. This time, a messenger bird appeared landing on his outstretched arm. "Take this to Captain Urdel" he instructed after tying the message securely to the bird's leg. Yuen then put his hood up like A would and started to guide his horse towards TeraKyla.

CHAPTER SIX

Death Upon You

TeraKyla celebrated with complete and utter jubilation. For months, their small town and people had been terrorised by Atdroc and his ruthless gang of bandits. Once the local Garrison had more than fifty members, but most had been cut down in their prime thanks to the men who were more merciless killers than simple bandits.

It was suspected that the elixirs they took not only enhanced their strength but affected their minds as well. It was the only explanation the town's residents could think of. Now, it was over. Atdroc was no more, and they had been saved by the most unexpected of heroes. Simple travellers who just happened to be in the right place at the wrong time.

For that, the citizens of TeraKyla welcomed them with open arms. Cheering as they walked the streets and cried out their thankyous to their heroes. One woman, heavily pregnant and close to sobbing with joy, begged to know their names so she could name her unborn child after one of them. Safe to say, the three were rather blown away at the immense gratitude they were receiving.

Especially A who Trisk noted was starting to look panicked at all the attention he was being bombarded with. Mercifully, the three plus Clovis were led to the Town Hall in the centre of TeraKyla. At the door, a Kaligan in a silken tunic informed them that their Town's Mayor would like to meet with them in private. Inside there was also the town's doctor who saw to Trisk's injury.

The leadership systems throughout Endonia changed from location to location and were convoluted, to say the least. Places like Ryu had a Lord designated by the Kaligan Royal family themselves to rule over, while smaller places such as Riven and TeraKyla had Mayors or simply followed the Garrison's orders if there was no such person in charge. Some cities had broken away from the Kingdom entirely, establishing their own, if unofficial, monarchy. Though in fact, there were only two true Royal families within Endonia. The Havenfall family represented the Kaligans, and the Camiré family represented the Pangarians. It was said that only the two Royal families could broker peace permanently between the two races. If the families could ever stop fighting amongst themselves, that is.

"Please, make yourselves comfortable" ushered the Kaligan with urgency "Our mayor does not like to be kept waiting. Your cloaks if you please" he said holding his arms out for said items of clothing. Mari and Trisk handed theirs over, but A was hesitant.

His identity was still hidden from the townspeople, and he wanted to keep it that way for as long as possible. The Kaligan continued to stare at him expectantly. Trisk nodded, silently saying that it was ok. Relenting, A removed his cloak and handed it to the Kaligan.

To his credit, the other man did not visibly react to his appearance. Instead, he quietly murmured "Ah. That explains a lot" before walking out of the room. The trio had been led into the office of the Mayor. It was a small but brightly lit room with a desk littered with unfinished paperwork. Some important documents were attached to TeraKyla, and others were pleas for help to other settlements. Upon closer inspection, Trisk could just feel the desperation the Mayor was feeling while writing these letters. All of which had come back with notices that help was not coming.

"No wonder they were so happy we arrived," he said to the others "According to these papers, that Atdroc fellow had been terrorising this place for months"

Mari shook her head sadly "Gods, those poor people. I can't even imagine how scared they must have been going through that"

On the other side of the room, A was glancing at the bookcase that was filled with books from all over Endonia. Books A couldn't read. For such a small office, the bookcase took up half the room and was near bursting with the amount of literature resting on its shelves. "Wait, is that the tales of Bubly and Finkle?" Mari asked suddenly at his side. She pulled the book free and smiled brightly "It is! I haven't read this since I was a kid" She turned to him still smiling "What about you? Anything here tickles your fancy?"

It was an innocent question but one that had A looking downcast at the floor "About that... I can't read. Or write"

Mari blinked for a moment then let out a groan "Oh boy, I sure keep putting my foot in it, don't I?" she facepalmed at her ignorance "I'm sorry. I keep offending you"

"No, no. It's ok. I get it" A responded. Thankfully, they were saved by the door to the office being opened. In walked a very large and very exhausted-looking Borgan who had to bend down to get inside. The moment he saw them, however, he was beaming like a little child on Yule Day. Before any of them knew it, all three were swept up in a massive hug that was almost bone-crushingly tight.

"Thank you" was all the Borgan said, emerald eyes shining with unshed tears "Thank you, for saving my people"

Trisk wheezed "Don't... mention it...!"

With a chuckle that just exuded happiness, he set the trio down. "Truly, I cannot thank you enough. That man was a menace and needed to be dealt with. TeraKyla owes you a great debt. All of you" the Mayor pointed a look at A but it was of sincerity, not disdain. "Please, if there is anything we can do for you, just say the word"

"Well, two of our horses bolted during the ambush" explained Mari

The Mayor cut her off "Say no more. I'll have some of my men go out and find them. If we can't

I'm sure we can rustle up some from our stable. As for tonight, I insist you stay at our local inn. It's not much to look at, but I can promise it'll be a comfortable stay"

"Oh, Sir. We couldn't-"

"Please, call me Langnir" the Borgan with the kind eyes and bearded smile spoke

Trisk coughed "Langnir. We couldn't possibly accept. I'm afraid we need to get to Marden within the fortnight"

"My, that is a trek you plan to make" he examined all of them from head to toe, including little Clovis who was sniffing the ground by the rug. "Still, I hope you take us up on the offer. We are eternally grateful for what you all did for us"

"Well, to be honest, A did all the work," said Mari with a pointed thumb to the Half Breed next to her "Trisk and I were just lucky to get out unscathed"

Langnir appeared impressed at the news "Well, my thanks to you, A. and I genuinely mean that"

"...It's fine" A mustered out in a quiet voice

"Sir?" the servant from earlier poked his head in through the gap of the door "Some of the townsfolk wish to speak to you"

Langnir chuckled "No rest for the wicked, I see. Please excuse me. I'll have Cylen here bring you something to eat while I'm gone. I shan't be long" he exited the office with a spring in his step. The three were left to their own devices for a short time until the Kaligan servant returned with a tray of steaming hot tea and a litany of deserts and pastries.

"Thank you very much" Mari said smiling brightly taking the offered tray which seemed to catch Cylen off guard. He too left them alone. "Dibs on the tiny cakes"

"Fine by me. I just want something with coco in it" Trisk said grabbing a coco-filled pastry off the tray "A? What do you want?"

A came closer to the tray to examine it. He started to reach out for one of the many treats when his hand froze mid-reach. They both turned their heads to him only to see he had a faraway look in his eyes. It was over in a second and A backed away from the tray as if it might burn him. "...I'm good. I'll just have something to drink" he mumbled pouring himself a cup before walking to the other side of the room. Trisk was confused and Mari was concerned.

"That was weird, right?" she whispered to Trisk who nodded in agreement, mouth full with specks of brown around his mouth. Across from them, A slowly sipped at his tea, his mind miles away at that time. He didn't even notice Clovis at his feet, whining to get his attention. He remained that way until Langnir returned sometime later. The Borgan was still smiling but somewhat unsure that time around.

"So," he announced "It appears you've been invited to a little party"

"Party?" repeated Trisk while Mari appeared perplexed, and A turned his head startled.

✻ ✻ ✻

Yuen tied his horse up next to a midnight

black one which he regarded with an impressed nod. He found that in the short time it took for him to reach the town of TeraKyla, the town had transformed entirely. Lanterns strung from house to house, music played joyously in the town square, and anyone he could see had either beaming smiles on their faces or were happily talking to each other.

Hardly anyone over the age of maturity did not have a drink in hand. It dawned on Yuen just how terrified these townsfolk must have been. He could still see the remnants of makeshift defences around the town itself and the houses' meagre attempts of barricading. From what he had known of Atdroc and his brutality, Yuen could only imagine just what they had been through.

Their trauma was made all the more prominent when a group took one look at his imposing stature and nearly jumped out of their skin. It took Yuen showing them his Guard insignia to prove he wasn't a threat. The soldier was then given a tankard of sweet wine and welcomed.

"Took you bloody long enough" one citizen grumbled but refilled his tankard when most had been spilt when a few of the drunker townsfolk bumped into him. Yuen was soon practically dragged to the town centre where some of the people were performing a merry gig. He was plopped unceremoniously in front of the performers and then they left him be. Yuen stared at his newly filled tankard.

"Well... that happened" he stated to himself then downed half his drink in one hit. He felt like he was going to need it to get through the night. From his position, he could make out the group of travellers he had been instructed to follow. The Scan, the Half Breed, and the woman who had only joined them recently. They were next to a Borgan Yuen did not recognise but seemed like the average, kind-hearted Borgan to him. If his toothy grin and boisterous laughter were anything to go by. His attention fell on the lone Half Breed who appeared to want to be anywhere else at that time.

Like so many others, Yuen had believed Half Breeds didn't exist. That their existence had been entirely made up. With so much animosity between the two races even to this day, though the intensity varied from place to place, Yuen would never believe one could exist.

Yet here he was staring at one with his own eyes. Yuen couldn't help but feel uneasy. He could just tell that the man across from him had not lived an easy life. The way he held himself, both to stand tall and to protect himself at the same time, was enough of an indicator. Which was why Yuen was uneasy. Why had Urdel ordered him to follow this man? What good would come of it?

He was brought out of his train of thought by a loud yap at his feet. Yuen glanced downward and found himself staring into the eyes of what was probably the most adorable puppy he'd ever seen. His little tail wagged away and his tongue hung out as it panted. Yuen remembered the rations of dried seasoned bore he had in his satchel. He fished two pieces out and held them up "You want some?"

Clovis barked

"Alright, here you go" he threw them to the ground which Clovis gobbled up within moments. He then tilted his head up expectantly "Sorry. No more" Clovis whined but then trotted off towards A and the others. Yuen realised the dog was also part of their group which only surprised him further. Yuen shook his head and finished his drink. He would think about it in the morning.

Before him, the performers finished their song and received a round of applause from everyone in the vicinity. The main performer, a Pangarian around Yuen's build with thistle purple hair, announced loudly "And now, a word from our Mayor"

"Thank you, everyone," he said when the applause died down "First, I want to thank our guests of honour this evening. Without these fine individuals, our home would have been lost to the bandits. I can only apologise that I was unable to gather help before" he admitted, solemn-faced "And so, please join me in thanking the new heroes of TeraKyla" the gathered townsfolk began clapping which only grew with every word Langnir spoke "Today, we mourn our lost brethren, but we also celebrate that their deaths have been avenged. May the Gods bless them!"

The crowd cheered "May the Gods bless them!"

"May the Gods bless them" Yuen whispered under his breath. Though he was conflicted, he could not deny their actions had saved TeraKyla from a fate unimaginable to most. He could respect them for that. As the celebrations continued well into the night, one soul wandered out of town and into the nearby forest. His path ahead lit only by a torch in his hand. He was barely fifteen, of short white hair and pointed ears.

His parents had instilled in him that he was to never go into the forest. However, now that the threat was gone, young Aaron disobeyed the instruction. He wanted to go see Atdroc for himself and hopefully spit on his corpse. It was because of the bandit leader that Aaron lost his older brother. Aaron needed to see him dead with his own eyes. Only then would he be able to work through the loss of his brother.

He made his way towards where the ambush had occurred. His hometown growing smaller with each step forward. Aaron understood that there were still many dangers lurking in the woods, but his need for closure pushed him ever forward.

He could deal with his mother's wrath when he returned home. After trekking some distance, Aaron came across splatters of blood on the path. Soon he came face to face with the body of his brother's killer. Atdroc, who had tormented his home for months and had taken his brother away from him, was indeed dead. Aaron breathed out a sigh, the heaviest of weights lifting from his young shoulders. "Done in by a Half Breed of all things" he commented shaking his head "Well, I'm glad someone finally got rid of you" Aaron fulfilled his wish by spitting on the corpse "That's for my brother. May the Four curse you, Atdroc. I know I will"

As he turned to leave, a hand covered his mouth. His torch fell from his grip as he was dragged away into the shadows of the forest. His terrified gaze glimpsed one of the men start to pick up Atdroc before he saw no more.

Back in the town, the celebrations were still going strong. Trisk had stepped out past TeraKyla's borders to get some air when he saw a familiar horse come galloping towards him. Even in the dark, Trisk could recognise the animal anywhere "WindRacer?" he asked aloud "What the – where did you come from?" he managed to grab the reins pulling them so the horse would come to a stop. That's when Trisk began to yell "Oh my - Mari! A! Get out here, quick!!" Trisk's shouts had gained the attention of some of the townsfolk who were in hearing distance. When they caught sight of what Trisk was shouting about, all thoughts of celebrating vanished in an instant.

Mari was the first to arrive "Trisk? What's going -?" her words died in her throat as her hands came up to cover her gaping mouth. A came into view moments later only to reel back at what he was seeing.

"Holy..." he nearly swore, the colour draining from his cheeks. Sensing something was amiss, Langnir made his way to them. His once cheerful demeanour vanished when he saw just what the cause of their panic was. Atop the horse, attached by crudely tied rope, was the bloody lifeless body of the young Kaligan.

"AARON!" came the heart-stopping wail of his mother. Two Kaligans shoved their way through the building crowd of horrified spectators. Aaron's mother all but collapsed in grief at the sight of her youngest son's body, wailing sobs cutting through the hearts of all around. His father was no better, nearly catatonic seeing his boy like that. "Oh Gods, no! Don't take him as well!" the mother pleaded to the Gods that remained silent to her plight.

In the back of the crowd stood Yuen, his face pale and shoulders tensed. He was unable to speak or even move. He'd seen enough death in his career as a Guard, more than he should of. He had believed himself used to it. Even desensitized. He was wrong. Seeing the boy not much younger than he was when he joined up slaughtered was enough to chill his blood. Yuen felt the mother's pain deeply. It reminded him of his own mother's cries so many years ago.

Aaron was cut loose and set gently on the ground where he was swept into his sobbing mother's arms. That's when A noticed the latter pinned to the dead teen's chest. "May I?" he asked the mourning Kaligan softly. Between heaving sobs, she nodded, and A removed the letter. The corner was red with Aaron's blood. "Trisk, what does it say?" he asked handing the letter over to the Scan. Trisk quickly examined the words and felt his stomach drop.

"Well? What does it say?" pressed Langnir

urgently

Trisk cleared his throat before speaking *"To the residents of TeraKyla,"* he read the letter aloud *"We demand reparations for the death of our leader, Atdroc the Vile. His death will not go unpunished. We demand what supplies you have left and all wealth in your treasury, or we will do to all of you what we did to the boy. We will return tomorrow at sundown. This is your only warning"*

The crowd openly panicked at the dire threat.

"But we can't give them anymore!" one man declared "We're barely scraping by as it was"

"They'll kill us all anyway" another said frantically "We all saw what they're capable of during the raids. They won't just settle for what little we have left. They want blood!"

Langnir stepped forward "Please, please, everyone. We cannot lose our heads just yet. We need to come up with a plan"

"What's the point?" muttered Aaron's mother with tears still streaming down her face "They killed both my sons. What's stopping them from killing us all? There's no hope…"

Suddenly, a voice from the back announced loudly "There's always hope" The crowds parted to show Yuen making his way forward. He came to a stop in front of Langnir. "There is always hope" he repeated

"And who are you? You are not of TeraKyla" the Borgan asked with an air of suspicion

"I am a member of the Capital's Royal Guard on transfer" Yuen explained, careful not to give his name away "If you allow it, I will help defend your people. By my honour and my sword, I swear it"

Langnir seemed placated "And what can you do? I admire your fortitude, but you are only one man"

"It won't be easy. I've seen what monsters like these bandits can do. But if we work together, we will make it through the night" Yuen turned to the gathered crowd, the entirety of TeraKyla. "I know I am a stranger to you. And I understand if you do not trust me. But I give my solemn oath, that I will fight to the bitter end to keep you safe. As a member of the Guard, it is my duty to protect and serve those in need"

Much to Trisk's disbelief, A spoke up "And you'll have my aid" he announced with a glint in his eye.

Mari added "And mine" she said glancing at her newfound friends

The Scan gave a sigh and a shake of his head before speaking " I can't believe I'm saying this, but count me in too"

Soon enough, all were pledging themselves to the fight. Including those who could hardly stand or those far too old or young. Friends of Aaron and his brother the loudest of the gathered people. Yuen placed his fist over his chest and bowed in respect. He looked back to Langnir. The Borgan gave a single nod. They would not yield. They would fight.

CHAPTER SEVEN

Preperations Made

Yuen didn't say a word as he threw his belongings into his woven sack. In the other room, he could hear his mother weeping. He tried his best to ignore it while deciding what to take and what to leave behind. Yuen understood why his mother wept, but he also knew he couldn't stay. Not when no one else was willing to do what he would.

He placed the last item in his sack, a purse containing what little coin he had earned working the fields. Yuen slung the sack over his shoulder and paused to gaze at his childhood bedroom. Two empty beds barren of their owners sat across from the other along with a weathered chest of drawers and patchwork curtains hung on the open window.

He let out a long sigh, one filled with sadness and longing. With one last look, Yuen left the room entirely. He stepped into the small living room of his home where his mother sat in her chair next to the fireplace, face in her hands and still crying while her husband tried to comfort her. It broke Yuen's heart to cause such pain but he was steadfast in his decision. He had to go. The Pangarian youth made it halfway to the front door when his father called for his attention. "Are you satisfied now, boy? Look at what you've done to your poor mother"

Yuen shut his eyes and took a moment to calm himself. The last thing he wanted was to leave home with bad blood. "Father, you know why I have to go. You of all people should understand" he answered, imploring his father to see it from his perspective.

"The only thing I understand is the pain you're causing to your family" The older man now stood inches away from Yuen. Towering above him as only a father could. "Yuen, please. Don't do this. There's no point"

That one sentence made Yuen's blood boil. He took a sharp intake through his nose before responding "I'm sorry you feel that way. But I'm leaving regardless of what either of you thinks"

From her seat, his mother wailed "Yuen, no!"

"I'm sorry, mother. I truly am. But I'll never be able to live with myself if I don't at least try" the son said with deep sadness in his dark eyes. His mother could only cry more at his words. Yuen glanced up at his father "I'll take my leave. I'm sorry"

"Yuen…" spoke his father, much more pleading this time around "Please, don't do this. Yuin… She's gone. It's already been a year since… Do you want your mother to lose you as well? You're all we've got"

Yuen spun on his heel to face him "I refuse to believe she's gone! I refuse to do nothing while she's still out there!" he turned his back on his parents once more "Goodbye father" he stepped over the threshold and into the sunlight.

"It's hopeless, Yuen. There's no point chasing a ghost"

Yuen shook his head defiantly "There's always hope" With that, Yuen walked away with heavy shoulders and a heavy heart. But deep inside, Yuen was sure he was making the right decision. Everyone else had given up so easily after Yuin disappeared. Not Yuen. Never Yuen. Yuen would never give up on his other half. He'd gladly spend every waking moment of his life searching if it meant a chance to find Yuin. That day, he made a promise to himself. No matter what, he would find his sister.

❊ ❊ ❊

"How many people reside in TeraKyla?" questioned the Gard overlooking the map of the town. Once it had been decided that they would stand and fight, Yuen had been brought to Langnir's office to figure out their next move along with what was left of the town's Garrison.

"At last count, just over three hundred souls" answered Langnir "I regret to say that Atdroc was very thorough in his dealings"

Yuen took that information in "And how many bandits?"

"We counted maybe sixteen during the last raid. Not including Atdroc and his right-hand man, Reika" one of the members of the Garrison explained

The lone Guard's jaw clenched. Like Atdroc, Reika had his own infamous reputation. Not as bloodthirsty as his counterpart but more than dangerous enough for Yuen's taste. It shouldn't have surprised him that Reika would throw his lot in with someone like Atdroc. He also didn't find it surprising they had resorted to illegal methods in order to ruin the lives of others.

He could only hope that the Bandits knew what they were doing and hadn't taken too much. Yuen had seen just what an overdose could do to the mind. "What about their supplies of elixirs? If we can cut them off at the source, that will benefit us majorly" Langnir winced openly, along with several of the Garrison members "What is it?" questioned Yuen

"I'm sorry to say this, but... we think the elixirs might be coming from someone in TeraKyla" the Borgan announced with deep shame "The first time they raided, they attacked all of us equally. After that, they left one home unbothered. Our town Healer, Paros"

"Scum is what he is" muttered one man angrily

"We don't have any proof he's involved with them, but you must admit the circumstances are very suspicious"

Yuen nodded thinking it over. Healers took a vow to help and care for those sick or dying. For a Healer to instead aid in those who cause such suffering, made Yuen feel sick to his stomach. "I understand. We'll deal with him later. Right now, we need to get this place fortified" he leaned over the map of the town, inspecting it intently. "We'll have men placed here, here, and here" he pointed to the various places on the map.

Outside, the panic had subsided but only just. Mari and Trisk watched as young Aaron was taken back to his home, his mother wailing as they did. "Bring him home" was all she could say through her tears "He needs to be home" Much to their shock, A had stepped forward and offered to carry the teen to his house. Without complaint or even a word, A carried Aaron through the streets of TeraKyla, cradling him with a softness neither of his newly acquired comrades had seen.

"That poor woman" Trisk said sighing

"I heard Atdroc killed her eldest a few weeks ago" whispered Mari almost curling into herself "I can't imagine losing both children like that"

Trisk had to agree. He had no children of his own and didn't plan on having any either. But he could agree that no parent should have to suffer the loss of a child. Let alone both children so close to one another.

The mourning parents and other family members lead the way to their home. It was a quaint small house painted a sunny orange with brown window frames. Still carrying Aaron, A was granted entry inside. Another wave of tears overcame the grief-stricken mother and she fell to her knees just as she passed the doorway.

"His bed" she choked out "He - it's past his bedtime..." Aaron's father was in no better state. The man had barely spoken a word since it happened, but it was clear that he was just as broken as his wife. A nodded and an aunt of the family offered to take him to the room Aaron had shared with his brother. A set Aaron down on his bed and closed his glazed-over eyes. If not for the blood, he would have appeared simply asleep. A wasn't sure what drove him to offer his help in bringing Aaron home. Well, that wasn't true. It was part guilt and part long-buried memories that forced his helping hand.

"Thank you" said the aunt with a sad smile "I can't believe this is happening. I didn't think the Gods were so cruel to take both children away from my sister"

A shook his head "No Gods were responsible for this. Just the actions of men who don't value the lives of others" he finally looked away from the teen "I should go"

"Wait. Let me fetch you some clean clothes. I don't think my sister could stand seeing you covered in her son's blood" A glanced down at himself and realised his shirt was covered in bright red blood. The Aunt wandered off to find something for him to wear, and A stayed back in the room. His pale blue eyes ended up staring at the deceased boy. A felt a sense of hopelessness he hadn't felt in years.

It was dark. So, so dark. He couldn't breathe. He couldn't escape. He pounded his fists on the fallen rock, hoping desperately that someone on the outside could hear him. "Help!" he cried "I'm still alive down here!"

Then he heard it. Someone's voice screaming from the darkness "A!" they screamed for him "Please, help me!"

"Here you go" the aunt said returning, jarring A out of his thoughts "I hope this will fit. Sorry, it's the largest I could find" she said handing him a freshly cleaned green linin shirt. A shook his head slightly to rid himself of the memories then took the offered clothing.

"Thank you. I'll take my leave now" After changing and hiding the blood-stained shirt on his person, he made his way down the stairs. There he saw the gathered family comforting the grieving parents. A chose to just head for the door. He didn't want to bother them in such a trying time. He made it to the door but was stopped by a broken voice coming from the sitting area.

"Atdroc deserved what he got," the mother said, red-rimmed eyes and tear-streaked cheeks "But it shouldn't have cost my son" She glared at A with all the anger a broken-hearted mother could muster "I should hate you for causing this. Gods know I should, but... Aaron wouldn't have wanted that" She turned her gaze to the floor "Just leave"

A didn't say anything as he left. When the door was shut behind him, he let out what could only be described as a wounded noise from deep within. He was no stranger to death. If anything, death was an old friend to A by this point. But this? This was too much.

He slid back against the door until he landed on the ground. Despite how awful he felt inside, he refused to cry. No tears would be shed. That promise he would keep. Gathering himself, A got back to his feet. There was work to be done after all. He walked back to where Mari and Trisk were. Clovis padded towards him snuggling against his ankle. "Hey. You alright?" Mari asked concerned

"I will be once we deal with these idiots" he grabbed his cloak which Trisk had been holding for him. "Just give me something to aim at"

❃ ❃ ❃

Morning broke but no one in TeraKyla had slept a wink. The incoming danger far too pressing for anyone to rest when time was of the essence. Yuen took charge of giving the men and women in the town a crash course in how to defend themselves, while those who were unable to fight were helping reinforce the barricades and build something of a defence against the oncoming attack. Yuen had the Garrison bring whatever spare armour or even practice armour they had and distribute them so the people would at least have a fighting chance.

The only blacksmith in town, whose stores had been raised bare weeks ago, was working as fast as he could to produce what weapons he could on such short notice. Burning the wick at both ends throughout the night and well into the morning.

In the middle of all this, the travelling trio involved themselves in whatever way they could. It seemed that in the face of certain danger, no one cared that A was a Half Breed. Either too concerned with what was to come or just too busy to notice. A was gathering wood to help reinforce the barricades. Trisk was inside the town hall with Langnir attempting to figure out if there was anything the town could give the bandits without allowing TeraKyla to starve.

Mari made herself useful by keeping the

children of the town calm and otherwise occupied. Playing games with them inside the town hall or singing songs to entertain them. She always had a soft spot for children and no one their age should see their parents so worried. She was playing hide and seek with them, her being the seeker, when Trisk exited the office looking downcast.

"No good?" she asked when their eyes met.

Trisk shook his head despondent "They've already given or had stolen what little they had. If we give up anymore, they won't last the winter"

"Then we better win this for them" Mari declared passionately "You any good at fighting?"

"Not exactly. Fighting was never my strong point"

Mari looked at the main entrance "Maybe ask that Guard fellow for some advice. Maybe even A if he's available"

"Good idea. Hey, you stay safe now, alright?"

"Same to you, Trisk" she responded shaking his hand as a good luck gesture.

"Miss Mari?" a small voice called from down the hallway

She called back "I'm coming. I gotta go. Good luck out there"

Trisk waved her goodbye. He then exited the building. Just outside the Hall, Yuen was training several citizens in the way of archery, using piled-up sandbags as makeshift targets. Some had the talent, others didn't. Trisk narrowly missed getting hit by another arrow when one of the trainees sneezed. "Sorry about that" Yuen said on the other's behalf "You any good at archery?"

"Never tried. I'll take a lesson though"

"Good man. Follow me. We'll get you started" he led the Kaligan to the others and handed him a bow and one arrow "First thing to perfect is your stance" he showed Trisk what he meant by standing in the right position, arms miming the action of pulling back a bow string. "Remember. Position and pose, and you won't go wrong"

Trisk attempted to mimic the Guard. He aimed

his bow at the sandbags which had been painted with sloppy targets, then fired. The arrow hit slightly to the left but was the closest any of the other men managed to get. Yuen grinned brightly, half with relief that there was at least one decent archer he could work with. "Well done, my friend" he congratulated. Trisk was dumbfounded that he managed to even hit the sandbag at all. "Don't worry. I'll make an archer out of you yet"

Meanwhile, Langnir had tracked down A to accompany him when he confronted the town's doctor. The Borgan would have waited for Yuen but realised the Guard's training of his people was far too important to interrupt. Langnir also had a few choice words for the good doctor that did not require a Guard to be in attendance. So, he asked if A would like to be there. Given what A had seen Aaron suffer through, the Half Breed was more than willing to accompany the Borgan. The doctor was hiding out in his practice, found between a residential home and a small tea shop which sold tiny cakes along with fancy teas. Though the window display had been emptied for some time.

Langnir knocked on the door "Paros? Are you inside? We need to talk to you"

They received no answer but heard the skid of a chair across wooden flooring. Borgan and Half Breed glanced at each other, both nodding in silent agreement. Langnir used his arm and impressive strength to break the door down, lock and all, giving the two men access inside.

The lower floor had been made into the doctor's practice while the upstairs remained his living quarters. The downstairs was split into two rooms. The front where the patients were treated and the back room which Paros used as storage and kept his equipment there. They stormed into the back room where they found a pair of legs kicking wildly as their owner tried to escape out the back window.

Langnir dragged him back inside with little effort needed. A discovered that the doctor was a Pangarian. He was older than him by several years, the vibrancy of his seafoam green hair fading at the temples. The man was broad wearing a traditional Doctor's brown coat on top of his usual attire. The back room was devoid of any storage or medical equipment.

Instead sat dozens of cauldrons bubbling away with testing tubes and scattered ingredients abound. Paros didn't even try to escape. He knew that the townsfolk would turn on him the moment he left the building for what he did.

The Borgan shook his head in disappointment "I had hoped the rumours were wrong about you" he announced

Paros couldn't look him in the eye "I'm sorry, Langnir"

"Yes, well... sorry won't bring back those we lost. Do you realise your actions helped those animals destroy our home? Put everyone in danger?" annoyed that the man before him refused to meet his eye, Langnir grabbed the man's chin to force him to look "They took your wife" he reminded the doctor coldly "They killed her. And you dishonour her memory by colluding with her killers"

Paros wrenched his face free and jumped to his feet "You think I wanted to help them? Langnir, I had no choice. What they did to my wife, they... they promised to do the same to my daughter" the Pangarian man admitted with sunken shoulders "My wife... my dear Myra...I can still hear her screaming as they dragged her away. I'm tormented by those screams every night. Don't you see?" he hissed, tears in his soft grass green eyes "I won't let my child suffer the same fate as she did. So, I agreed to give them the elixirs in exchange for protection"

"Well, a child died regardless of your deal," A told him with a stern expression "They killed Aaron, and are going to slaughter the lot of you tonight. Whatever deal you had with them, it died with Atdroc"

Paros was in tears by that point. The guilt of his actions eating him alive "Papa?" a small voice from upstairs called

The doctor quickly wiped his eyes "It's alright, sweetheart. Go back to playing" There was a pause of silence before footsteps were heard walking away from the stairs. Paros sighed "Look, I know I've screwed up. And nothing is going to change what I've done. But Langnir, please. Let me fix this. Let me do something to make this right" he pleaded.

A had to admit, the other man seemed genuine in his remorse. He could understand how the man could justify his actions. He may have been the town's only doctor and had a duty to his patients, but he was also a father desperate to save his only child. No matter what he chose, he'd lose either way.

For a tense moment, Langnir was silent. Contemplating his next words "You want to fix things? Fine. First, you are to destroy whatever is left of this lab of yours," he gestured to their surroundings "And if by some miracle we survive this night, you and your daughter are to leave TeraKyla at first light. For good"

The other man nodded emphatically "I

understand. Thank you, Langnir" With that settled, both Langnir and A were about to leave when Paros stopped them "Wait! I believe I may have a way to help you tonight"

"Go on" Langnir said slowly

"Most of these elixirs the bandits wanted are dangerous in more ways than one. They're also highly flammable" he explained grabbing a bottle of sparkling blue liquid to show them "I heard you were building barricades around the town, right?" A nodded in response "We could use these to light them on fire and give the bandits pause. Long enough for our people to strike"

Langnir hummed "It's certainly an option. They won't see that coming"

"Wait..." A interrupted "How much of this stuff do you currently have on hand?"

"Collectively? Roughly three barrels worth"

A continued "And how much could you produce by sundown?"

Confused, he answered "Um... maybe eight? Ten

if I used everything I have left"

"What are you planning?" questioned Langnir curiously "I hope you're not suggesting we use the same awful concoctions those brutes are using"

A shook his head "No, but I have an idea. "Paros, start brewing. Langnir, find me some shovels. We're going to dig a trench"

"Trench?" he responded with a splutter as A rushed out of the building "Why on Endonia would we need…" It suddenly clicked for Langnir what the Half Breed meant. He let out a shout of a laugh "The man's a bloody genius!"

"He's a bloody maniac, is what he is" Paros corrected but still began collecting the ingredients strewn across his lab.

Langnir laughed regardless "Perhaps. But it's mad enough to work"

He left the building and went to find Yuen to inform him of the plan. The Guard was impressed and somewhat taken aback with the absurdity of the plan. So absurd it just might be successful. As Paros brewed and townsfolk dug the trench around the town, preparations continued all around until the sky began to turn orange. Sunset was upon them. With no time to spare, the barrels were emptied into the dug-up trench. The colours of the foul-smelling mixture swirled as it was poured. Just one spark would create a ring of fire that the bandits could not avoid.

"Everyone who cannot fight, into the Town Hall. No one is to leave until I give the order" Langnir announced with a loud voice. His usual cheery demeanour was gone in preparation for what was to come. Before she headed for the Hall, Mari hugged Trisk and A goodbye. Wishing them luck and promising they'd meet in the morning. Clovis hung back by A's feet. Whining and peering up with a pining gaze.

A shook his head "Go with Mari. They need you more than we do" The small dog didn't seem pleased with the order but followed it nonetheless. His tail was low and still, as he went after Mari.

"Well, this is it," Trisk remarked trembling slightly "I have to say, defending a town from bandits is not what I anticipated when I asked to join you"

A shrugged "Think of it this way. If you survive, you'll have plenty to write about in that book of yours"

The Scan chuckled slightly "I suppose you're right" his gaze turned to the slowly darkening sky, orange ever so slowly fading into the dark blue night sky. Trisk swallowed back his growing fear. He had promised to help, and he would. Even if it meant he wouldn't see another sunrise. He felt Trindle would be proud. "Good luck, A"

"Good luck, Trisk. See you in the morning" he awkwardly patted the Kaligan on the shoulder as he walked away to his assigned position.

Trisk let out a nerve-wracked sigh when A left. He didn't want A to see him nervous. Not when so much depended on them.

Taking the last moment of peace he'd probably

have, Trisk reflected on what got him to this point in his life. Had he known following a Half-Breed would lead him to defend a helpless village from destruction, well, Trisk would like to think he'd help regardless of how he got there. "May the Creators watch over us all" he whispered as the day turned to night.

CHAPTER EIGHT

Fight For TeraKyla

As darkness fell, TeraKyla fell silent as well. Candles were blown out. Lanterns dimmed. Fires dampened. So dark one could hardly see their hand in front of their face. Those who could not join the fight hid themselves away in the cellar of the town hall. The entrance hidden under a rug and stacked empty boxes.

Inside women, children, the sick and infirm could only wait in anxious anticipation. There was no way out other than the trap door they had gone through. The cellar was not big enough to hold everyone, so only the most vulnerable were able to hide inside. Those who couldn't hide themselves away in their homes and could only hope for the best.

Mari lit a few candles to not leave them in total darkness. Some held out candles with thankful expressions while others held their children close instead.

"Mama?" a little voice questioned. It was a young Pangarian girl with soft lavender hair and small stature. She was clinging to her mother's skirt who was holding her newborn in her arms "Where's Papa? He should be here"

Her mother paused, swallowing back her fear to put on a brave face for her young daughter. The truth was her husband wasn't coming back, for he had been killed in the last raid and she had yet to find it in her to tell her daughter the truth. "He'll be here later, sweetie. He's gone to help the Garrison to get rid of those nasty bandits"

"Like a Knight?" the girl asked excitedly. Her mother nodded which seemed to satisfy her. Her mother then instructed her to go sit by her friends for now while she tended to the baby. When the daughter was out of earshot, Aaron's mother spoke up.

"You shouldn't lie to her like that"

The other mother frowned deeply "What was I supposed to say? She's scared enough as it is"

"And lying to her is any better?" the Kaligan woman asked with narrowed eyes wet with tears. Much more quietly, she said "You're only delaying the inevitable"

"One of us should have at least some hope" the purple-haired woman responded coldly "And who are you to judge my parenting? I don't see any of your children" It was a low blow and those in the cellar knew it. Thankfully the younger children were more preoccupied with their little games than the adults arguing.

Aaron's mother went beat red with anger "Say that to my face. I dare you" She stood up from the crate she had been sitting on ready to fight the other mother when Mari stepped between them.

"Enough" she warned loud enough for everyone to hear "Look, we're going to have enough fighting above us as it is. Let's try to keep things civil down here. Whatever issues we have can wait until morning. Now please, cool it" she was firm in her words but gentle with her gestures. It was enough for the women to cease their arguing and walk to the opposite sides of the cellar to cool off. Mari sighed retaking her place on the floor against the stone wall. She went back to stroking Clovis's fur to ease her growing anxiety. "This is going to be a long night"

Clovis ruffed in agreement.

Above them there was nought but the wind blowing gently through the leaves. In their scattered hiding places, most were too nervous to even breathe at a normal rate. Yuen and Trisk were ducked behind the stable giving a clear shot of the trench. The smell was unbelievable, and it made Trisk's eyes water. "Remember," Yuen whispered "Wait for my signal. We want to get as many of those bandits in one hit"

Trisk nodded "Where's A?"

"A?" Yuen questioned "Oh, you mean the Half Breed? I've got him on the wings as back up" They fell silent once more, both pairs of eyes fixed on the treeline in the distance waiting for any sign of the oncoming attack. "Where did you even pick up one of them, anyway?"

Trisk shrugged "Actually it's the other way around. We met in Ryu not too long ago. He saved my hide and I decided to tag along for a while"

The Guard blinked surprised "Huh. Not what I was expecting" They heard rustling and the hairs on their arms raised in alarm. Yuen peered through the gaps of the stable and could just make out movement coming from the forest path. "Here they come"

Gulping, Trisk steadied himself and aimed his bow and arrow. Though Yuen had faith in the Scan, Trisk wished he could find some faith in himself. His hands trembled. Sweat began to bead on his forehead. Trisk's eyes widened as hulking masses descended from the tree line.

"Trisk, now" Yuen ordered "Light the arrow and fire" but Trisk found himself paralysed with sudden fear. The reality of their, quite frankly, hopeless situation, crashing down upon him. "Trisk!" the Guard snapped quietly

"Come on, Trisk" murmured A from his vantage point, concerned he had yet to see anything from the gates.

Yuen sighed "Oh, forget it" he then snatched the bow and arrow off Trisk and shoved the Scan out of sight for good measure. He set the arrow tip wrapped in an oil-soaked rag alight, aimed, then fired. For the approaching bandits, the arrow barely registered. After all, what damage could one lit arrow do to them? They were puzzled when the first few Bandits ended up stepping into what they thought was water up to their knees. Until the arrow also landed in the water and all they could see was fire.

The flames spread until TeraKyla was surrounded by a wall of yellow and orange fire. The cheering of those able to fight didn't drown out the agonising screams of the Bandits who had fallen for their trap. From his position, A sighed in relief that his mad plan had worked. Part of him had feared the mixture wouldn't catch alight or that Paros had betrayed them one last time.

Two of them never made it past the wall of fire. Another four massively built Bandits came running into the town engulfed in flames and begging for mercy. Their pleas went unheard. For that night, TeraKyla would repay the cruel bandits in full for what they did.

"Attack!" came a cry from the shadowy forest.

"Charge!" Boomed Yuen with his sword raised high. "Show 'em what you're made of!"

With that, both sides descended upon the other. The remaining bandits leapt through the flames and over their fallen brethren, voices thundering into the night. Turns out Langir had been mistaken. Reika had called for reinforcements. Now instead of a dozen for face-off, there were over fifty.

Despite this, those defending TeraKyla beset them back with everything they had. Townspeople alike jumped from their hiding spots wielding whatever weapon they could get their hands on. Swords, maces, farming equipment, kitchenware. Anything and everything that was at hand for them to defend themselves. With their own trembling shouts of anger, the people showed no mercy to the Bandits that had tormented them for so long. Enough was enough.

Though the Bandits had the advantage of the elixirs given to them by Paros which increased their strength and ferocity, they found themselves to be completely outnumbered. Before the people wouldn't dare to fight back against them. Led by a Borgan who valued peace and virtue over anything else, it was no surprise TeraKyla hadn't put up much of a fight in the months leading up to this night. However, emboldened by Yuen's words and enraged at the losses they had suffered, they would no longer bow to the Bandit's whims. Atdroc's death had been the turning point but not in the Bandits' favour.

One by one they fell. Overwhelmed by the sheer multitude of furious and at times bloodthirsty townsfolk who at that moment, wanted nothing more than to erase the Bandits from existence. Armed with a dagger in each hand the Blacksmith had given him, A held his own against the enemy. A's life had been a hard one, there was no denying that, but A could pride himself in knowing he'd never resorted to becoming like the men who so cruelly brought TeraKyla to its knees for no good reason at all. He allowed his past anger to fuel him, allowing him to take down another one of the brutes with a swift swipe across the throat with his blade. He wiped the blood off his leg and continued onwards.

While outnumbered, one Bandit did manage to evade the townsfolk long enough to reach the town hall. He was a giant of a man even without the use of elixirs, with fists like mallets and teeth of tombstones.

He shoved his way inside the building, finding

it void of life but he suspected differently. Below his feet, no one even breathed. Mothers covered their children's mouths; the candles were swiftly blown out. Mari clutched Clovis to her chest in hopes the action would keep the pup quiet. She put her finger up to her mouth, urging them all to keep as quiet as physically possible. For a moment they couldn't hear footsteps above and a twinge of hope began to build that they hadn't been discovered.

Then a fist the size of a dragon egg broke through the floorboards and into the cellar. Screams burst from terrified souls all around. The fist lifted away and the Bandit's twisted grin peered down from above. "There you are" he said with the floorboards creaking ominously under his weight. He suddenly let out a howl of pain when a sharp broken broom handle was shoved straight into his eye. The weapon was wielded by none other than Aaron's mother.

"Everyone get out of here" she ordered clambering out of the hole "This bastard is mine"

The mother she had previously been arguing with let out a shocked scream as her fellow townsfolk disappeared.

"This way, come on!" Mari shouted; she and two other women using all their strength to open the hatch to the cellar "It's not safe here!"

One woman cried "What about Laila?" indicating to Aaron's mother

"There's no time! We've got to protect the children!" another shouted over her, sweeping up her daughter in her arms and clambering up the ladder. Mari had been the first out but had not left the Hall. She had positioned herself so that should the Bandit turn his attention on the women and children, she'd be the first to die. She aided the hysterical people out of the cellar. Taking children in her arms so their mothers could climb out unhindered. All the while Laila fought with a strength only a broken mother could wield. Using whatever she could grab at hand she fought back the Bandit with everything she had.

"Ok, that's everyone" Mari muttered to Clovis as the last person climbed out of the cellar. She heard a deafening scream come from behind her. Laila was clutching her side with one hand, red blood dyeing her dress at a rapid rate "Miss Laila!"

The Kaligan winced glancing towards Mari "Run" she spoke simply "No more children die today" She then lunged once more at the Bandit with a rage like no other. Mari swallowed back her guilt of leaving her behind, but Mari would be of little help against the Bandit either. She grabbed Clovis and bolted to the Hall's main entrance. Outside she stepped into what could only be described as pandemonium.

"By the Four..." she whispered in dismay seeing TeraKyla fall to ruin around her. The ring of flames bathed the town in shades of gold and orange. Sparks flew as sword met pitchfork, as cleaver met dagger. All around people scattered in desperation to find somewhere safe. All while bloodthirsty Bandits cut down anyone in their path.

"Mari! Down!" A shouted. Mari ducked just in time to avoid an axe to the skull. She tumbled to the dusty ground, staring up at yet another Bandit. The Four seemed to pity her at that moment, for her new Half-Breed companion threw himself onto the Bandit knocking him to the ground. With several fast stabs of his dagger, the bandit fell still. A, splattered with blood, ran to help her up to her feet. "You were supposed to stay in hiding" he said almost scolding her.

She pushed her golden hair out of her eyes "We were! One of those bastards found us!"

A then pushed them both out of the way as a hail of arrows narrowly missed them. "Look, you've got to find somewhere to hide"

"Sod that" the Pangarian proclaimed marching back to the Bandit's corpse and grabbing his fallen weapon, a massive greatsword at least the size of Mari herself with a green-toned handle and made of sage silver. A's jaw nearly dropped when she lifted the sword without even breaking a sweat "Just point me at the nearest ass that needs slaying"

A shook his head as she headed off out of his line of sight "Note to self. Do not get on her bad side"

❉ ❉ ❉

They were winning. One by one the Bandits dwindled in numbers till there were only two left standing. TeraKyla had suffered losses as well, but they had so far come out on top and were close to finally ending the nightmare. The last two bandits standing were battered and bruised, bloody and broken. It seemed only a matter of time before they fell just like their brethren.

Sensing the shift, one of the bandits desperately shouted "REIKA!" calling out for their now Defacto leader. He had been a step below Atdroc and was named leader after his death but had remained out of sight throughout the battle. Yuen had expected this. There was always one waiting in the wings to strike at the last moment. He quickly silenced the shouting Bandit with a swift stab through the chest.

Leaving one lone Bandit left in all of TeraKyla and one more somewhere in the forest.

The ground shook beneath their feet as they heard what they thought was a rumble of thunder. But the night sky was clear of any such oncoming storm. Birds and other forest creatures began fleeing the forest as the ground shuddered again. This time knocking some right off their feet. Getting back to his feet, Yuen moved to the ring of flames that still surrounded the town but had dimmed just slightly. Through the dancing flames he saw it, the Guard felt true fear for the first time in many a year.

"Guardsman?" questioned Langnir

"...Retreat"

"What?" the Borgan asked shocked

Yuen then shouted "Retreat! Everyone, get away from the fire!"

"Oh Gods..." the lone Bandit muttered with wide eyes "What has he done to himself?"

That's when Reika made his appearance. With every step, the foundations of TeraKyla were rocked viciously as he came closer. Not willing to let this be his last, Reika had done the unthinkable and consumed every last elixir he had left. Something only a madman would do when his back was against the wall. These glittering liquids should never be consumed at the same time.

The results were catastrophic for his body. He walked through the flames like the fire wasn't even there. Wide yet beady eyes scanned those at his feet far below him, looking for the fear in their eyes. Mammoth in size; he dragged his lumbering limbs behind him, swiping at whatever was in his way be it building or person. Not only had the elixirs morphed his body into something monstrous, but they had also warped his mind until he had but one thought left.

To kill.

"Gods above..." said Trisk both in awe and in horror.

"Everyone, get back!" Yuen ordered pulling out his sword from his sheath "I was trained for this. I'll handle him"

Langnir shoved him out of the way, taking the greatsword off Mari and turning to the monstrous brute. "No, Guardsman. You've done enough for my people. This fight is mine"

"Langnir, no!" someone from the town gasped "You're a Borgan. It's against everything you believe in"

The larger-than-life man came to a stop and so did what was left of Reika "This is all my fault. For bowing to their whims instead of fighting them head-on. I want you all to know... that I was honoured to be your Mayor" he shot them all one last smile, the same smile he gave his townsfolk every day, before charging at Reika with a mighty roar. However poetic his sacrifice might be, Yuen could not in good conscious leave Langnir to fight alone. So, he brought out his sword yet again and followed the Borgan into a battle for the ages. This time the townspeople stayed well back out of harm's way. Facing Bandits was one thing but going up against what became of Reika was another matter entirely.

Reika's movements were laborious and slow but packed a mighty punch. This gave Langnir and Yuen the element of speed on their side but Reika outmatched them entirely with brute strength. His hits when meeting their targets were like sledgehammers to bone. Langnir was the first to fall, with Reika managing to grab him with his tree-stump-sized fists and throw him out of the bounds of TeraKyla. Leaving Yuen to face him alone.

Brave souls offered to help but Yuen refused to let them interfere. After all, he was trained for this. He dodged the swinging appendages by the skin of his teeth. The Pangarian Guard managed to get a few good swipes in with his sword before getting knocked to the ground, only managing to avoid being crushed at the last second. He scrambled to his feet and charged at Reika once more, who only moaned out his grotesquely deformed mouth in return.

Still, the once Bandit gave no quarter and neither did Yuen. Eventually, Yuen realised his sword was no match against the hardened skin of Reika. So, he abandoned his attack and made a beeline for the greatsword Langnir had dropped.

This turned out to be a mistake. Reika took this opportunity and with a trip of Yuen's feet, managed to grab the Guard in his fierce grip. "No, no, no!" Yuen gasped as he was lifted into the air. Only it seemed Reika had different plans for the Guard. He lifted Yuen high into the sky. Dangling the Pangarian right above his oversized head. The gaping mouth opened wide, the foul stench of churning elixirs escaping like fog into the night. Reika then howled in confusion as something smacked him in the face.

"Come on!" Mari ordered loudly, arms full of debris and broken objects of all kinds "Throw everything you got at him!" soon enough, Reika was being pelted with whatever the townsfolk could throw at him. Some had even climbed atop nearby buildings to get a better angle. In all the madness, Reika dropped Yuen. The Guard landed hard on the ground with a loud thud yet he wasted no time in grabbing the greatsword this time. With weapon now tightly in hand, Yuen weaved through the falling debris, using what strength he had left to run up Reika's fallen arm to get a higher vantage point.

Once at the perfect spot to strike, he did just that. Leaping off into the air, he let out a triumphant roar as he forced the sword into the mauled chest of Reika, the blade going deep enough to pierce his engorged, overstrained heart.

Reika wailed to the heavens out of pain, his bulging legs giving out from under him. The corrupted Reika collapsed to the ground in a heap with a thunderous crash, taking out two nearby buildings with him. For the next few agonising moments, the people waited. Waited for him to die or rise and start his rampage once more. In the end, his twisted body couldn't withstand such an injury, and Reika's life faded with a final exhale of rotten air.

It was over.

However, before it could even begin to set in that the nightmare was at last over, Yuen suddenly fell to the floor in a dead faint. The sword crashed to the ground just like him.

"Paros!" A shouted into the crowd "Somebody find the doctor, quick!"

"Shit, that's a lot of blood" a Kaligan citizen who had rushed to help announced with a grim expression. Both Mari and Trisk knew a little healing and so came to the aid of the fallen Guard. They quickly came to realise these injuries were well beyond their abilities.

Paros pushed his way through the worried crowd. Leather medical bag in hand for good measure "Out of the way, let me pass" he demanded pushing passed the last of the concerned people. He unintentionally reeled back at the sight of him. Blood was pooling beneath him at a rapid rate and his amber skin was pale and already sweaty. He knelt beside the other man and felt where the blood was pooling out of him. He gravely shook his head "Get him to my house immediately. I need to fix this before he bleeds out on us"

Dozens of townsfolk rapidly volunteered to bring him to Paros's home. They made a backboard out of a fallen tavern sign and carried the unconscious Yuen away. The flames around the town burnt well into the morning. Signalling to all who witnessed the flames that TeraKyla would never bow down to anyone ever again.

In the chaos of getting Yuen help, no one noticed the last bandit make his escape out of TeraKyla.

CHAPTER NINE

Seed of Doubt

In the past, Rei liked to consider himself a good member of the Garrison. Once he was a shining example of what it meant to protect and serve the public both at home and on the battlefield. Even at his youthful age, he'd seen enough fighting and spilt enough blood to last him a lifetime. Perhaps it was his disillusioned mindset after returning home that caused him to be susceptible towards Urdel. Borgans were known throughout the land as kind and gentle with not a cross word to be uttered about another being. So, when Urdel took him under his wing, Rei thought little of it. Assuming like everyone else Captain Urdel was a good and just man who prided himself on doing good.

Oh, how wrong he had been.

It had started small at first. Rei wanted to impress his Borgan superior like any other good soldier would. It had earned him a reputation as a boot licker among the rest of the men, but Rei didn't care. Urdel had stepped into a sort of fatherly role for him, and Rei's own father had walked out when he was just a child. Too young to remember his face but old enough to remember the pain. Urdel used this to shape Rei and later Desmond into his trusty right-hand men.

Willing and able to complete any task handed to them, however unpleasant. In the end, Rei had become no better than the criminals he helped punish. Protected only by the Garrison uniform and his connections to Captain Urdel did he not face the same fate.

Things slowly began to shift for Rei when Urdel ordered that they arrest one of Riven's oldest citizens. His name had been Adlassan, once the town's most popular blacksmith who had retired due to losing the use of his left arm. Urdel had said the old man had been caught stealing and needed to be brought in for questioning. Like always, Rei followed orders. Adlassan claimed innocence but Rei refused to listen to the old man's plight. The next day, Rei learnt the truth. Adlassan hadn't been stealing anything. He had just failed to pay up his tab at the tavern. Whose owner just so happened to be a good friend of Urdel.

When Rei discovered this, he went straight to the cells to release Adlassan for his wrongful arrest. Sadly, Rei instead came across the man's body being taken out of the cell for burial. Adlassan had died that night under mysterious circumstances which Urdel quickly had swept under the rug.

This death was the beginning of Rei's shaken faith in Captain Urdel. He kept his mouth shut for the next few months but watched closely with eyes no longer blind. What he saw made his blood boil and his skin crawl.

Bribery, extortion, black market trading, just to name a few things. He kept an extensive list of everything he found out along with any names he suspected of being involved. Rei understood this would lead to his career being ruined and almost certainly imprisonment, but Rei was steadfast. He would stop Urdel in any way he could. When a member of the Royal Guard arrived in Riven, Rei believed this was the turning point. He could give his gathered information to Yuen who could in turn take it straight to the capital. Only Udel had Yuen sent off before Rei could even talk to the Pangarian.

Rei didn't expect only a day later to be ordered to saddle up his horse and follow said Guard. Something was brewing and Rei didn't like it.

❋ ❋ ❋

"Just admit it. We're lost"

"We are not lost!" defended Rei while he tried to make sense of the map he was holding "If anything, that bloody Guard got us lost" he muttered "Why would he take a left back there? That doesn't even lead anywhere"

Desmond shrugged "Well, he was following orders just like us. Maybe he needed to take a detour. The woods aren't exactly safe, you know"

Rei barely registered what his comrade was saying. He kept staring at the map hoping it would magically tell him the way they should be going. It wasn't his fault Yuen had taken a detour after all. He was still boring holes into the map with his eyes when they both heard a rustle coming from their left. Their location meant any number of hostiles could be coming their way, so neither man hesitated to pull out their swords in preparation.

From the brush staggered a Kaligan man drenched in sweat and filth. His feet bleeding through his boots from how long he had been running. The man managed a weak-sounding plea for help before collapsing by the two men's feet. Rei and Desmond re-sheathed their weapons and went to help the fallen man.

"What happened to him?" wondered Desmond aloud

Rei winced "Look at his feet. He must have been running for days to get to that state" he shook his head "Poor sod. We should probably get him back to camp. Have someone take a look at those feet"

"Good thinking. Help me pick him up, will you?"

With some struggling, they managed to get one arm slung over each of their shoulders. The camp was roughly a thirty-minute walk in the opposite direction they had been walking. Urdal had insisted the entire group keep going but some of their fellow Garrison were literally falling over from exhaustion, so Urdal reluctantly agreed to pause for the night. Rei and Desmond, however, had been instructed to scout ahead to see the path Yuen was taking.

"What do you think Urdal is up to?" Rei braved the question after some internal debate.

Desmond sighed "Not this again. Look, just keep your head down and don't question your orders. You'll live longer"

"Well, you have to admit. He's being damn suspicious. Letting the Half Breed go, ordering the

Guard to follow. Then ordering us to follow?" Rei shook his head with a sour expression "I don't know, something feels rotten about all this"

His colleague and frankly, only true friend, rolled his eyes "Well, I'll let you be the one to confront Urdel. Just warn me beforehand so I can get out of range"

Silence fell between them till they reached the small camp. It was set up in a small clearing that had recently been hacked away for firewood. The fire pit burned brightly in the middle of the camp. Garrison members, a dozen in total not counting Rei and Desmond dotted the area. Some still in full armour. Others half-dressed ready for a proper night's sleep. All chatter and noise quieted down when Rei and Desmond appeared, dragging along between them the Kalagian they had found.

One Garrison member who was the most adept at healing came towards them to help. He and Desmond took him to one of the bedrolls. Rei rolled his shoulders and sighed, only to be met with Urdel staring down at him with bulging crossed arms and curled fists. "I thought I told you to track Yuen's movements"

Rei glanced at the campfire where the Kaligan man had been laid out. "He needed our help"

"I gave you... an order" the Borgan stated coldly. Despite the fire being close by, Rei felt a chill go up his spine. He wanted to say something in defence of his actions but thought better of it. Desmond's earlier warnings rang clear in his ear.

On the bedroll, the man returned to the waking world but was delirious with exhaustion and fatigue. He began mumbling under his breath. Words that were a jumbled mess of subconscious thoughts. Urdel was uninterested until the man started mumbling things that grabbed his attention. "St-stop the Guard..." the man mumbled tossing fitfully in his delirium "Don't - Don't let... H-H-Half Breed..."

Suddenly, Urdel was very much interested in what the man was saying. "Out of the way" he pushed Desmond out of the way to get closer to the Kaligan. "You. What is your name?" he was met with more stuttering mumbling. "Where did you come from?"

"Tera...Kyla..."

Urdel hummed thoughtfully "What happened there? Why did you run?" he pressed further "Answer me!" he snapped when the man couldn't string a sentence together.

"He - He killed him..." the man whispered "The Half... he killed Atdroc..."

Filling the camp was a resounding gasp. They all knew the story of Atdroc and his vile deeds. Of the horrors he left behind wherever he went. One of the most wanted criminals in Endonia. Now he was dead. Killed by the Half Breed no less. The very thought seemed impossible to Rei. He'd met the Half Breed in person. The other man hardly put up a fight against only two Garrison officers. For him to down one of the worst bandits Rei had ever heard of? It must just be mad rambles. However, when Rei glances up at his Captain, the gleam in his eye tells a different story.

"Get this man some water" Urdel announced standing back to full height. "Once he's coherent, bring him to my tent"

It would take roughly a half hour before the man, who they eventually learned was named Herius, was fit enough to speak regularly. Sat up against a tree, Rei observed with a pensive gaze as Herius was escorted to Urdel's tent by Desmond.

Again, he had that sinking feeling in his chest. He couldn't say why, he was just sure that Urdel was planning something. The minutes ticked away causing Rei to grow restless. His dark purple eyes would dart towards the tent where he could make out no noise or movement. He tried to remain patient, but he eventually grew tired of not knowing.

No one else seemed to think anything was amiss, not even Desmond, so Rei quietly picked himself up and walked towards Urdel's tent. As the Captain, it went without saying he would have better accommodations than his subordinates. The tent was made of clean and coloured canvas made from recovered sails. As to not alert suspicion, he grabbed a bottle of wine before going inside so it looked like he was simply bringing Urdel a drink.

"Captain? I brought you a -"

His boot squelched when he stepped inside. Rei froze mid-step, his gaze slowly moving downward to see what lay under his boot.

Rei's stomach lurched when his eyes met the sight of Herius lying motionless on the ground. The man's head caved in almost completely. "W-What the -" he backed away only a step before the foreboding figure of his captain loomed over him. One fist had red blood dripping from it and the other held a sword that was dwarfed in his larger hand. "C-Captain...?"

"You should have just gone back on the road, Rei. You'd have lived longer"

Rei ran. He stumbled out of the tent legs shaking

with fear. He could have run back to the campsite. Back to his friend. But for all he knew, they would turn on him on Urdal's order. So, he burst into a sprint into the darkness of the surrounding forest. He had no weapons, no way of defending himself. His only way of survival was flight.

He kept on running. Weaving through the blackness tumbling over tree roots and sprinting until his lungs cried out for air. Eventually, Rei jogged to a stop. Doubling over to catch some much-needed breath. The man glanced around, seeing nothing and hearing nothing. Then darkness truly fell upon him when a massive hand grabbed his head from behind and dragged him further into the forest.

❈ ❈ ❈

Desmond snorted awake. Eyes fluttering open to dim sunlight hidden by an overcast sky. He had been rudely awoken when one of the men dropped his spear next to the sleeping man. The rest were already awake and packing away everything. He had slept next to the firepit on a bedroll which wasn't very comfortable. He yawned moving to sit up, stretching to get the kink out of his back. "Morning, rei" he greeted as usual. Only Rei did not respond. He looked over and found Rei's bedroll already packed away for that day's trek. Desmond frowned in confusion. Rei never woke up before him. "Where's Rei?" he asked a passing Garrison.

The other shrugged "Beats me. Captain Urdel said he left camp hours ago. Heard he turned back to go home"

That made the hairs on Desmond's neck prick up "He did?" climbing to his feet, Desmond went in search of Urdal. He found the Borgan captain helping with the teardown of the camp for the next leg of the journey. "Captain?"

Urdel boomed a laugh "About time you woke up" he joked "You sleep like the dead, son. I was half expecting to have to leave you behind"

"Captain, where's Rei?" pressed the Pangarian

trying to hide his unease

Urdel didn't even hesitate to answer "Rei came to my tent last night complaining of illness. Something up with his stomach. So, I sent him homeward. Told him to take that Herius fellow with him as well" he finished off with a grunt as he lifted three wrapped up tents onto his shoulder. Desmond followed him as Urdal walked to one of the supply wagons.

"But he was fine last night" continued Desmond, his worry starting to bleed into his voice as it cracked slightly while he spoke "And he would have at least told me he was leaving" Around him, those Garrison officers close by started to drift away suddenly finding anything else much more interesting.

Urdel sighed not even looking at him as he tied down the tents so they wouldn't roll off during travel "It was the middle of the night, Desmond. You were asleep. I'm sure you can understand"

The Pangarian's lip curled into a frown. He

breathed out through his nose "I should go follow him. He may need help"

"No need for that"

"But if he's sick enough to need to go back home then surely, he's sick enough to need an escort" he explained turning around to go get his things.

Urdel's voice cracked like a whip "Desmond" he spoke simply, but his words held a weight to them. One that would no doubt be weighing on Desmond soon enough. "Rei is perfectly capable of travelling back alone. It's just a stomach bug. He'll live"

"But-"

"That. Is. Enough" the Borgan stated, swiftly ending any conversation between them. "Now get your things. We'll be setting off when the horses are ready"

Desmond felt his heart grow heavy with unease. Something was wrong, he was sure of it. But Urdel showed no sign of deceit or suspicion. What if he was wrong and Rei truly had just gone home, and he was making a fuss over nothing? In the end,

Desmond unclenched his fists "Yes Sir..." he agreed begrudgingly, walking away to grab his sword and satchel.

"Alright, everyone. We're losing daylight. Let's move!" Ordered Urdel taking the lead at the front of the line. Desmond lingered at the campsite till he was the last man standing. He stared down at the spot where Rei should have been that morning. With a shake of his head and another exhale of warm breath, Desmond followed his comrades. Followed Urdel.

At the front of the line, Urdel wore a smile on his face. This was not unusual for Borgans. It was rare to find a Borgan who didn't smile at least three times an hour for no reason at all. For Urdel, it was uncommon to see him smile amongst his men or even out in public in general. Still, he smiled for he knew what was to happen next. How that blasted Half Breed would no longer escape his just punishment. How he would be richly rewarded by Lord Callum when all this was done.

How he would finally be rid of his nuisance of a brother.

CHAPTER TEN

Aftermath

A gagged as he scooped up the mixture into the bucket. The fabric covering his nose and mouth did little to mask the foul smell. "This is disgusting"

"Well, it was your idea" commented Trisk trying not to vomit wearing the same kind of fabric. They along with other townsfolk were cleaning up the remains of the battle. The most arduous task was what was left of Paros's concoction surrounding the town. The mixture had to be collected in buckets and then transferred to the waiting barrels for disposal. After seeing what happened to Reika, no one in their right mind wanted anything to do with the stuff.

A rolled his eyes "Hey, it worked, didn't it?" he

gagged again. "Urgh, this is awful" he gladly walked over to one of the barrels and dumped the contents inside it. A paused to look around "Where's Mari?"

"With Paros helping the injured. That Guard is lucky to be alive after last night"

The Half-Breed hummed "Given the circumstances, I think we should all be a bit grateful" he then sighed shaking his head "What about those hiding in the Hall? How many got out?"

"Most got away unscathed. Though... Aaron's mother sacrificed herself to make sure that everyone got out" the Kaligan said with slumped shoulders. "Poor woman" Though his movements were awkward, A patted Trisk on the shoulder as a gesture of comfort. Trisk smiled appreciatively. "Come on. The sooner this mess is cleared away, the sooner we can get back on the road"

"In a hurry to leave?"

"In a hurry not to miss our deadline" he clarified "No offence to the man but... Urdel kind of scares me"

A couldn't quite argue there.

Meanwhile, Mari was tasked with accounting for those who were injured and those who didn't survive the night. She shed a few tears when Aaron's mother was brought in, her body covered in a blanket. She had bravely given her life taking down the man that would have killed them without question. Mari's sadness was nothing compared to that of the grieving husband and father. Both children and wife were slain and he was powerless to do anything. She glanced up from her list to see said man sitting broken next to the fountain. His gaze was empty and no doubt his heart too.

"Here," she said after walking towards him. In her hand was some bread "You should eat something" He turned his gaze away. Silent tears ran down his cheeks. "Well, I'll just leave this here" he knelt to place the bread next to him. "Goodbye, sir"

"...She was pregnant" Mari paused mid-step, turning her head around "Only a few months, but... Paros believed she was carrying a girl"

Mari's heart clenched and broke all at the same time "Oh, I'm – I'm so sorry"

The mourning man just shook his head "You lot avenged them. You have nothing to be sorry for" he finally met her gaze. Mari could see the pain in his eyes as clearly as she could see the sun. "Thank you"

Throat clenching, Mari could only nod and make a hasty exit. To lose so much in such a short span of time, Mari couldn't even imagine how harrowing the pain must be. She took a moment in private. Away from the dazed and recovering townsfolk to compose herself. She needed to be strong if she was to be of any help to those who needed aid. Gathering herself once more, Mari returned to Paros's side to continue giving whatever help she could. Even if it meant simply bringing a smile to a face.

Back with the injured, Paros set down the knife with a tired sigh. He then covered the poor soul with a sheet. Another neighbour he was unable to save. He'd been lucky in the grand scheme of things. Only losing another two people that day after so much devastation. Though as a healer, it pained him every time to lose a patient. Especially when it was his actions that helped lead to their death. "Rest easy, my friend. May the Creators welcome you with open arms" he spoke a quiet prayer in hopes their spirit would hear it.

Mari came towards him "Anything I can do to help?"

Paros shook his head "No. I think I've got things covered here" he gave the young woman a small smile "You should go wash up. I'm sure your friends will be waiting for you"

"Alright. If you're sure" she responded about to walk away "Oh. How is that Guard doing? He looked hurt pretty bad last night"

"I won't lie, it was touch and go for a while. But he's a fighter" Paros told her while packing away his medical kit "He'll be out of it for a few days. He needs rest to recover fully. I doubt he'll be awake anytime soon"

Mari nodded "Well, give him my best when he does wake up. We'll probably have left by then"

"Will do. Thanks again, by the way,"

※ ※ ※

"And heave!" Langnir instructed. The men grunted with exertion as they attempted to move the body of Reika. Still horrifically deformed and enormously large, moving the body was a feat in itself. It took at least four men to lift one limb and even that was pushing their strength to the fullest. They ended up fashioning a winch to help lift the body out of whatever could be scavenged. Langnir had one of his arms in a sling and his people refused to allow him to help clean up. He'd given enough is what they told him. "Try again, lads. Heave!"

"Langnir" his assistant Cylen spoke coming closer, in his hand a rolled-up piece of parchment "Just received the last count from Paros. Most made it through the night but we lost two more people. I've informed their families"

The Borgan sighed "Considering what we all went through... send the families my condolences. Give them something towards the funerals. At my expense"

"Will do, Sir" The shorter man turned on his heel and walked away. Langnir paused to rub his injured arm with a wince. He'd regain full movement in time but for now, he just had to deal with the pain. Some pain was nothing he couldn't handle.

The winch snapped apart under the weight of the body with a thundering crash. "Is everyone alright?" the Borgan questioned

"We're fine. Trust this bastard to be a pain in the arse even after death" one of the men responded which caused a light chuckle to emanate from the other men.

"Well, let's try again" Langnir sighed "I want him out of here before he stinks up the place"

Back with A and Trisk, they had just finished their task and were taking a much-needed breather away from the disgusting stench. Masks down around their throats the two breathed in the fresh air gratefully in heaving gulps. "Oh, that's better" Trisk rasped between breaths "Creators, that stank to high heaven"

A nodded in agreement, eyes watering from the stench having stung his senses so badly "Remind me never to suggest anything that mad again, alright?"

The Scan shook with a snigger "Hey, it worked didn't it?" he said repeating A's earlier statement. A shoved at his shoulder.

"There you two are" smiled Mari as she walked over to them with Clovis in her arms. The puppy was sound asleep snoring away. His small legs kicked slightly in his sleep. "I'm finished up with the wounded. You guys finished too?" she then gagged suddenly "Good grief, you guys stink! What were you doing? Bathing in that mixture?"

"Very funny" A deadpanned

"Yeah, we don't smell that bad" added Trisk. He then smelt the collar of his shirt and his face scrunched up in disgust "I take it back, she's right" he blew out air through his pursed mouth "I'm off to the bathhouse" he turned to A "You coming?"

A shook his head "I'll bathe in the river" The Half-Breed marched off before either could say anything else.

Mari frowned "TeraKyla doesn't have a river" she spoke to Trisk who only shrugged his shoulders in response. He wandered off to find the bath house leaving Mari with Clovis in her arms. The puppy yawned before settling back down. "Yeah, you sleep little one. It's so hard being a puppy, isn't it?"

❊ ❊ ❊

The trio set off later that day. Waved goodbye by the townspeople at the southern gates. "You'll always be welcome in TeraKyla. All of you" promised the Borgan while giving each of them a one-armed hug which was still somehow nearly bone-crushing. Mari's original horse had been found and given back to her, much to her gratitude. "Feel free to visit any time"

"We'll hold you to that" Mari announced kicking her horse into movement. The two men followed suit atop their horses setting off as the afternoon sun shined down upon them.

Trisk glanced back at the gates where people were still waving them off. "What a night" he mused "Not what I signed up for, let me tell you"

"You kind of did" Mari corrected with a sly smile, Clovis on her lap yapping in agreement. "I just hope that Guard is going to be alright. He took a hell of a beating from Reika"

Trisk nodded "I'm sure he'll be fine. Warriors like that aren't down for long"

"I suppose" she sighed then frowned "Hey, did anyone catch his name?"

The Scan opened his mouth to speak but realised he didn't know either. "Huh. Guess I must have missed it. A?"

"Don't look at me. I just called him Guard"

the blue-haired Half-Breed responded shrugging his shoulders. The trio plus Clovis continued onwards. They had to make up for lost time if they were going to reach Marden in time. Trisk looked back once more, this time the town was far in the distance. There was a distinct expression of worry on his face.

Mari guided her horse closer to him "Hey, you alright over there?"

"Yeah, just... I hope we haven't made TeraKyla a target" he spoke with worry "No doubt news will spread about Atdroc's death. When word gets out what we did, that little town will be known to half of Endonia by springtime"

The lone blonde groaned "And here I thought we were helping, not making things worse"

"We did help" A cut in; face obscured by his hood once more "And if all goes to shit again, at least they know they can put up a damn good fight"

Mari smiled "I guess you're right" She gave Clovis's head a pet as she spoke "Though I doubt anyone would dare take on TeraKyla now. They'll be famous all right"

"How many days till we need to be in Marden?" Trisk asked A

A replied "We're a day behind but as long as we don't become wrapped up in any other mad situations, we should be there by the end of the week. Hopefully, this Rylon character won't cause us any trouble once we get there"

"Who is Rylon again?" questioned Mari

"Urdel's brother. We were tasked to bring him back to Riven so their father could see him again. He's dying" her companion told her "Captain Urdel paid quite a handsome sum for it too. Just a pity we weren't able to find it afterwards.

"How much?"

"Hundred gold as downpayment. Four hundred when we got back"

Mari openly gaped at him in disbelief. She glanced between him and A several times before smacking her forehead with her hand "Gods above, you two are idiots"

The Scan balked "Excuse me?"

"You two had a fortune hanging on your belt and you didn't think to hide it better? Not to mention the ludicrous amount of coin – hundred gold!" she scoffed

"Well, it's not like we intended on getting ambushed by bandits" defended Trisk glancing at A for moral support.

Taking pity on Trisk, A interrupted them "Alright, cut it out. Both of you. I'm dealing with this arguing all the way to Elayas"

"I am not arguing. I am just commenting on past events" Mari huffed "Elayas? I thought we were heading for Marden"

"It's the last stop between here and Marden. It'll take us at least four more days of travel before we reach Marden, so we'll need somewhere to rest before then"

"Ah. That makes sense" she agreed without resistance. Mari thought back to the events of TeraKyla. How she kept thinking back to the Guard who had saved them "I hope he's alright..." she whispered under her breath.

Meanwhile; back in TeraKyla Paros hovered over his last remaining patient of the battle. Yuen lay on the bed panting while he slept, mumbling nonsense as sweat beaded on his brow. He had been doing well for a while, but fever had taken route. Fever wasn't an uncommon symptom after such an ordeal on the body, but Paros couldn't help but grow worried when Yuen slipped into delirium.

That usually indicated he had developed an infection. The doctor had painstakingly removed Yuen's wrappings, re-checked his stitchings, and then reapplied the bandages but found no sign of anything amiss. If Yuen had truly developed an infection, then it was in his blood already. Something Paros couldn't fix. And so, he waited for the inevitable.

❈ ❈ ❈

Yuen opened his eyes to clear skies and

squawking birds flying overhead. The smell of wildflowers and crabgrass hit his nose. Familiar in such a way it made his eyes sting with tears. How long had it been? Ten years? Fifteen?

He opened his eyes once more, almost black irises blinking in the noonday sun. Something akin to a smile formed on his face as he sat upright. His eyes caught sight of a murky lake; its water nearly green in colour. Yuen hadn't seen this place in so long. He'd almost forgotten what it looked like. At the shore of the lake, with her arms wrapped around her knees, sat a girl with black hair gently moving in the breeze. Yuen felt his heart stop.

"Yu... Yuin?" he wondered aloud climbing to his feet. The girl craned her head back to see him. No matter how many years had passed, Yuen had never forgotten her. Had never once forgotten her face, her smile, her eyes. Forgetting her was something he could never do. Not while there was breath still in his lungs

"Yuin... Sister -" he stepped forward. Only a step

but was then suddenly routed in place. Yuen stared at his feet finding them to feel like they weighed more than he could possibly lift. He struggled to move even an inch but couldn't. "Damn it all... Yuin!" he shouted for his sister "Yuin!!"

Slowly, Yuin rose to her feet with a grace he wasn't familiar with. She hadn't aged a day. Not since the day he saw her last. She was still as young and youthful as she was back then. Yuen shook his head in defiance of the obvious. He wasn't dreaming. He wasn't going crazy. His sister was here. She must be. But her sad eyes gazing up at him told a much different story. "I'm dreaming, aren't I?"

Yuin nodded silently.

The older of the two sucked in a breath, struggling to accept that as fact. He wanted so badly for her return to be real that he was willing to ignore the obvious. "I see... Are you... Why are you here? I – I haven't dreamt of you in – in forever. Not since..." Yuin, still as silent as ever, turned away from him and pointed towards the opposite side of the lake.

There the dream began to twist in on itself. The surroundings of his childhood started to tremble and shudder rendering him nervous. "Yuin, what's happening?"

That's when familiar voices began to fill his ears. Quite at first, they soon turned into an unbearable cascade of noise ringing in his ears. Yuen fell to his knees clamping his hands over his ears in a vain attempt to block out the noise. He could vaguely make out the voices of his parent among the racket, though one voice, in particular, stood out above the rest.

"You know what needs to be done..." Urdel's voice rang out **"Kill the Half-Breed... Leave no witnesses..."**

"C-Captain Urdel?" Yuen gasped out before groaning in pain. He was hit full force with a searing pain emanating from his chest. He'd suffered many injuries over the years but this one by far hurt the most. "Yuin?" he looked up to find his sister only to see she was nowhere to be seen. His sister, or whatever image his mind had concocted of his sister, had vanished. Tears fell from his eyes. Both from pain and sorrow. "YUIN!" he cried out as his vision grew blinding "I'll find you! I swear it!"

❉ ❉ ❉

Paros was midway through mixing a new recipe when Yuen bolted awake with a shout. It made the other man drop his bowl out of pure fright, letting it smash onto the floor. "By the Four, you're alive!" he wheezed out after catching his breath. Yuen fell back onto the bed as agony ripped through him. "I was starting to think you wouldn't wake up"

Through gritted teeth and barely open eyes, Yuen managed a whisper "P-Paros?"

"Aye, lad. And if I must say, it's great to see you awake again. I was half expecting to call an undertaker"

Mind foggy with pain, memories of what happened began to filter back in. "The - The bandits..."

"All taken care of," the doctor promised disappearing from Yuen's line of sight "You were one lucky man. Your ribs were cracked, and your lung was punctured. I won't even comment on the amount of blood you lost" Throughout his tangent, Yuen could only breathe through the pain as best he could. His eyes snapped open when he remembered his dream. Paros was startled by a loud thud. Yuen had fallen out of bed and was gripping the old frame as he pulled himself up. "Sir, I must insist you get back into bed. You need rest"

Yuen shook his head "The Half-Breed. Where is he?"

"Why, he and his friends left days ago" Paros explained. Yuen felt his chest tighten even further. "They would have waited but they had an appointment in Marden – Sir, I really must insist!" the Doctor pleaded as Yuen, barely able to stand upright, trudged over to where his uniform was laid out along with his sword.

"No time" he spat, groaning while he struggled

to dress himself "Do you have Bluebird Milk?"

"Yes, but I can't give you any. You've already had two doses -" Paros was silenced when Yuen held a sword to his throat.

Yuen huffed an unamused smirk at him "Considering I should drag you back to the Capital for colluding with Atdroc and have you rot in prison, consider this an act of generosity. Bluebird Milk. Now"

"...Fine" Paros relented. Yuen lowered the sword and watched as Paros fetched three bottles of blue liquid from his cupboard. "Here. It's all I have. Two doses a day. Any more, and you'll overdose"

"Understood" Yuen swept the bottles into his satchel "Thank you, Paros. I'll be on my way" he managed to limp out of the house with Paros on his tail. Once outside Yuen shouted, "I need my horse!"

Hearing the commotion, Langnir came over to investigate "What is all this – Ah, Guard. So good to see you up and about" Yuen marched passed him grimacing with every step "Maybe not. Guard?"

He followed just like Paros who was now demanding Yuen return to his house as he was in no condition to go anywhere. Yuen didn't listen. He let out a pained cry as he mounted his horse. Yuen took the chance to catch some much-needed breath "Guard, where are you going? You can barely stand" Langnir questioned

"I have to catch up" he muttered taking the reins "Langnir, listen to me. Another Borgan might come this way. His name is Captain Urdel. If he passes through, tell him nothing about the Half-Breed" without warning, Yuen, kicked his horse into a gallop. He and his horse were soon out of the bounds of TeraKyla leaving only dust behind.

Langnir shook his head "You saw it too, right?"

"The glowing blue glint in his eye? Yes, I saw it" Paros sighed "Dream sight. Just what we need" Paros sighed. He glanced to his home where his young daughter was still upstairs packing. Langnir had allowed him to stay long enough to help the injured, but that time had now passed "I... suppose I should get going. Thank you, Langnir. And I'm sorry. For everything"

He made it all of two steps when Langnir called for him "Paros" he spoke making the shorter turn around "I don't agree with what you did. Helping Atdroc and his me. But I can understand it"

"What are you saying?"

"I'm saying that perhaps leaving is not the way to make things right. You've done much for TeraKyla these last few days. Perhaps if you stay, you can make up for what you did"

Paros couldn't help but smile at the offer "That's... thank you, Langnir. I'll consider it"

"Dream sight, eh?" Langnir muttered after Paros left, his gaze drifting to the road Yuen had galloped away on. "I wonder what he saw"

CHAPTER ELEVEN

Old Friends

"Are we there yet?" whined Mari, her voice taking on an annoyingly high pitch. A could swear she and Trisk were doing it on purpose to get on his nerves. They were four days into travel with Elayas only a few hours away. But the journey had been far from a blissful one. Trisk had somehow managed to get food poisoning on the first night which left the Scan very ill. Mari had offered to ride back to fetch Paros, but Trisk insisted it would pass on its own. They were delayed an extra day by the time he was fit enough to continue.

"Are we there yet?" Trisk joined in barely able to keep his eyes open. After Trisk was well enough to travel once more, they had made it a fiar distance before stopping for the night. that was where their

small campsite was ambushed by a curio
bear. It wouldn't have been so bad if Clovis h
gone on the offensive and set the bear off. The one
upside was that the trio ate well that night on bear
meat. Slightly gamey in taste but incredibly filling.

"No, we are not there yet" sighed A ushering his horse to go faster. The night before had by far been the worst. An unexpected downpour had all but flooded their campsite and they were forced to seek refuge in a dark spider infested cave. The spiders wouldn't have posed such a problem had they been regular sized spiders. considering the ones they had delt with had been the size of Clovis and bigger still, no one got any sleep that night. From his spot on A's lap, Clovis let out a long yawn. "Oh, *you're* tired?"

Trisk shook his head in an attempt to stay alert "That had be be the longest night of my life. I never want to see another spider again for as long as I live"

"I second that" Mari added with a yawn "Whoever decided spiders needed to be that big deserves a right kick up the bum"

uckle "I think that would be

ll stands" she retorted in jest.

o look past A on his horse "How much further do you think?"

A shrugged "Couple hours, give or take"

The chatter died down to silence as the trio's horses continued walking along the road. Though the more disused paths were safer to travel, they didn't want to tempt fate on the of chance Adtroc had other men hiding out in the forest. About an hour further down the road, they caught the sound of singing coming from a caravan that had parked up on the road. The wooden caravan was down a wheel and the horse that had been pulling it was tied to one of the nearby trees, The singing coming from inside the caravan was off key but no less jovial with every note.

"Looks like they've broken down" Trisk commented bringing his horse to a stop "We should help them"

A glanced at him incredulously "Have you learned nothing from these past few days?"

"Apparently not" he answered back, jumping off his horse to head towards the caravan.

A let out a withering sigh "Self-preservation skills of a squirrel, that one" which made Mari muffle a laugh behind her hand.

"Hello?" Trisk asked knocking on the door "We were just passing by and we saw your caravan had broken down. Do you require any help?" he spoke, albeit, shouted at the closed door so the occupants could hear him. The singing stopped but no one came to answer the door. "Um, hello?" Trisk asked again with another rap of his knuckles.

Trisk blinked and he was laying spread eagled on the ground having been thrown off his feet when the door to the caravan burst open with a blinding light "What the -?"

"Trisk! Are you alright?" Mari questioned as she and A lept off their horses to help the fallen Scan. Mari helped him to his feet while A took a defencive stance between them and the caravan. Blades in his hands at the ready in case of the worst. The blinding light lasted a few more moments before it vanished into nothing.

From the caravan's interior, they heard a man shout "Away with you, blasted noncussession of the stone!" out of the door came flying a dull yellow crystal which landed at A's feet with a skid across the ground "Test number fifty six... failure"

"Um... hello?" this time Mari called which managed to recieve a reaction from inside the caravan. Popping out of the caravan was a Kaligan man on the shorter side for his kind, thinning white hair and his fair share of wrinkles.

"What is it? Can't you see I'm busy?" he spoke in a cracked voice, teeth black as coal.

"No bloody way..." Trisk whispered before letting out a shocked laugh "Cassadore?"

The older man boomed a laugh so loud it almost send the birds in the nearby trees flying "Trisk!" he exclaimed "By the Creators, its been an age!" the man eagerly gestured for them to come inside "Come in, come in. I'll make you some of my famous black star tea"

"You know this man?" A asked re-sheathing his blades

Trisk nodded excitedly "This is Professor Cassadore. He was my mentor back at the Library. Well, till he tried to burn down the north wing"

"That fire was a set up!" Cassadre shouted from inside the caravan

Trisk smiled regardless "Let's go in. You two are going to love him. He's got the best stories you'll ever hear" A and Mari watched as Trisk entered the caravan.

A looked at Mari "I told you. Squirrel"

✽ ✽ ✽

Cassadore's laughter filled the cramped caravan while he poured the trio another serving of his tea. The tea itself was anything but black. It was bright red in colour which slowly turned pink once you added lemon juice to which Cassadore was insistent they ass to get the full flavour. Despite the lemon juice, it was a bitter concoction that only Cassadore seemed to enjoy. Cassadore had a small table in which all four were huddled around with Clovis dozing underneath between their feet.

Almost every free space in the caravan was covered in clutter of all kinds. Jars of preserved animals and insects filled almost every shelf. Any spot left was home to a textbook or an old picture. There was so nuch that there was hardly room for people to sit comfortably, let alone live in.

"You should have seen this lad in the Library. he was one of my best students in all my years of teaching. He could talk circles around any scholar this side of the country" Trisk became bashful under such praise "Though it does make me wonder. What are you doing do far away from Redencon? I thought I Scan such as yourself would never want to leave those pretty walls"

Trisk chuckled awkwardly under his old

mentor's gaze "I suppose your wanderlust rubbed off on me. After a while I just decided to head out and see what else the world had to offer"

"Good lad" he said approvingly "Don't make my mistake and spend your life buried in books. Being banished was probably the best thing that could have happened to me"

"Mari set down her untouched cup of tea "Why were you banished?"

"Cassadore scoffed "Bah! It was all a set up I tell you. I'd have never endangered the Library, no matter what anyone says. I swear they just wanted an excuse to boot me out. I was on thin ice with them for a while before that. Shouldn't have been surprised now that I think about it"

"Oh, I'm so sorry" she said in sympathy

"No need, dear girl. I'm far better off out hear. Now I get to do whatever I please. Within reson of course. Last thing I need is to wreak old Mildred any further" he said while patting the wall of the caravan.

"... Mildred?" questioned A with a raised eyebrow

"You name a horse, don't you? You name a dog, a place, an item of significance. Why should my humble abode be any different?"

A didn't know how to respond to that considering he had no name to begin with. He just remained quiet and nodded as if in agreement. While Cassadore splintered off into another story of his adventures, A's eyes fell on something peculiar sat on the shelf just behind the once mentor. He'd seen a lot of strange and weird things over the years, but this had to be a first. From what he could tell, inside a large glass jar appeared to be a grey fluffy cloud which was gently floating and bouncing against the glass. Tiny droplets of rain falling ever so gently down to the thin layer of soil inside the jar.

"Excuse me, but what is that?" he asked pointing behind Cassadore. The others turned to look at what A was pointing at. Mari had the same curiosity as A, Cassadore beamed proudly, while Trisk turned white as a sheet.

"Cassadore..." Trisk mumbled with an audible gulp "How did you...?"

Cassadore grabbed the jar and turned to place it on the centre of the table. Trisk backed away as far as his chair would allow him. "This, my friends, is quite possibly the most dangerous creature in existence. Or rather, half the creature is we're being specific"

The golden-haired woman peered closer almost pressing he nose against the glass "It doesn't look all that dangerous. kind of cute if you ask me"

"That it is" the older man agreed "However, once you make it anger..." he demonstrated by shaking the jar roughly in his hands. Trisk all but dove under the table for cover waking uo Clovis in the process. When the jar was placed back onto the table. the mice little cloud had turned into a full blown storm inside the glass gar. Tempered glass being the only thing from stopping the storm from bursting free. Even though it was small. they culd hear the howling winds and see the swirls of a tornado along with the flashes of lightning.

A was rendered speechless for a moment "That's incredible..."

"It's named many things. Most of which I can't even pronounce myself. In this stage its relatively harmless. It'll tear the roof off but that's as far as it will go" he explained in a joking manner. From underneath the table, Trisk dared to poke his head up to peek. He somehow became even paler and slowly sank back under the table clutching Clovis to his chest for comfort. "But if one of these storms crosses paths with a spirit, theres no telling what damage it will cause. That's when it becomes... the Galomorick Storm" he spoke its name and the storm strapped within glass thundered as if demanding its release.

"I've never heard of such a thing" Mari said now leaning back in her seat eyeing the jar with a wary gaze.

"I doubt you would have. Galomorick Stroms leave nothing behind once they begin their carnage.

Save for the lucky few who live to heed its warning" Cassadore put the jar back on the shelf ignoring the noises it was making "You can come back up now, Trisk. It's safe"

Trisk showed his the top of his head once again "Those things are supposed to be impossible to catch"

"Tell me about it. I caught that little guy back 1st year by the skin of my teeth and the skin of my backside. Call it skill or pure dumb luck" he shot Trisk a smile full of pride in himself "Tell me lad, are you impressed?"

"I'm starting to think you're madder than I first thought" answered Trisk. Cassadore let out a hearty laugh just as his hanging wall clock chimed the hour.

Mari turned and gasped "Is it that late already?"

"Oh great" A sighed "We'll be lucky to reach Elayas by nightfall at the earliest" he stood from his seat and headed fro the door.

"We should get going. It was lovely meeting you

Mr Cassadore" Mari said pulling Trisk back to his full height "Love to stay longer but we're running late as it is"

Cassadore shook his head "No need to apologise my dear. I'm just sorry I kept you so long. Trisk, don't be s a stranger now"

"I'll try!" he responded as he was yanked out the door by Mari with her hand gripping the collar of his shirt. At Casadore's feet, Clovis waited expectantly with his tail wagging and mouth panting. Chuckling, the Kalagin tossed the puppy some leftover steak. Clovis happily napped the meat in his mouth and hurried off after his owners.

"Cassadore waved them off "It was good seeing you again, Trisk. Hope to see you again sooner rather than later"

The younger man smiled taking the reins of his horse "I'll try my best, Cassadore. Just do me a favour. Get better tast in tea"

Cassadore's mouth hung open in mock outrage as Trisk and his companions galloped off "I don't insult your taste in fiction now, so I?!" he shouted after them. Trisk merely waved back with a laughing grin

"See you around, Cassadore!"

"That boy, I swear..." he sighed shaking his head fondly, smiling nonetheless. He then looked at where his caravan should be in possession of a wheel. "I really should get that fixed"

CHAPTER TWELVE

Bard's Beginning

Not many people passed through the gates of Elayas after nightfall which made being the night watchman quite a boring occupation. Still, the pay was decent, and the most trouble a watchman would have was the rare unruly individual trying to force their way through without a pass.

That night was different as well after the sun had set and the light of day gave way to starlight, a small group of travellers and a puppy on horseback of all things were at the gates asking for entry. Caeda was surprised to see one of his own travelling with a Pangarian without issue. Though the fighting had officially ended that didn't mean bad blood still didn't run true in the hearts of many. Caeda tried not to judge his fellow Kaligan but it was easier said than done.

"State your business" he spoke solely to Trisk

"Just passing through" he answered "We'll only be here one night"

Caera nodded jotting down in his records "Official Pass"

"Pass?"

The Watchman sighed "Only those with business, residential, or work passes may enter Elayas's boundaries. No pass, no entry"

"Show him the parchment" A voiced making Caera jump where he sat

"Bloody-! Where did you come from?" he asked the hooded man who didn't respond. Only met his gaze until Ceara was the first to blink.

Trisk pulled out the rolled-up parchment and showed it to the Watchman. He skimmed through its contents till he reached the name attached to the parchment "Urdel? The Borgan guy from Riven?" he questioned in surprise. He thought the parchment to be fake. Even held it up to candlelight to see if he could make out any mistakes or signs of fraud. He failed to find any "I'll be damned... Didn't expect this tonight" he handed Trisk back the parchment "Alright. You can go in. Just don't make any trouble while you're here"

"Cheers. Where's the nearest inn if I may ask?"

Caera gestured with his thumb "Follow the pink signs. You'll eventually find it"

Night had fallen hours ago by the time A, Trisk, and Mari finally made it to Elayas. The settlement, Too small to be called a city but too big to be classed as a town, was founded on the Elaysia River which is where it earned its name. Elayas was said to be blessed by the Gods to have fertile fields and forever blossoming bounties year-round. No one in Elayas went hungry and the settlement was famous for providing much-needed aid in the final stretch of the war. It was also said to be the birthplace of Endonia's first recorded dragon. Some say the dragon will return to its birthplace one day and its return will signal the end of time. Though that's what those who drink too much Elaysian burdock rootstock will tell you.

"It's prettier than I thought it be" Mari commented as they guided their horses to the stable. After night had fallen the settlement came alive with music, revelry, a bustling night market, and enough ale and wine to knock out a Borgan outright. Lanterns of soft pink lined the streets to match the ever-blossoming trees that were the markers of the settlement. The petals would fall softly to the ground where they would be piled up into large mounds in which children would play in. When the petals turned colour after some time on the ground, they would be turned into a sweet wine that was sold all across Endonia.

Clovis was already playing with one of said petals between his paws.

"Well, they've certainly embraced the pink aspect of this place" A said tilting his head all the frankly garish amount of pink buildings, street decorations, and even fashion choices. Not everyone wore something pink but it was enough to be a noticeable trend among the people living in Elayas."Hate to see this place in the rain"

Trisk was the last to secure his horse. He patted the mare on the side promising to bring her an apple in the morning as a treat. "We should find somewhere to stay for the night. Where's the nearest inn around here?"

"He said to follow the pink signs…" looking around, Mari saw that all the signs in Elayas were pink "Which is far from helpful" she noticed A secure his hood so it wouldn't fall off as they walked. Though she didn't know him well, it pained her to know he was forced to keep walls around himself just for some semblance of security. She and Trisk could walk freely without worry. I couldn't even do that.

"What?" the Half-Breed asked when he caught her staring

She shook her head "Nothing. It's nothing" She

bent down to pick up Clovis and hold him in her arms "Let's go this way" Mari took the lead with Clovis in her arms. She glanced at the puppy with a confused look "Odd. You weren't this heavy yesterday"

"He's a growing boy. What did you expect?" quipped Trisk which Mari responded with a roll of her golden eyes. They ended up in the night market made up off all kinds of stalls you could imagine. From dressmakers to antique dealers, from merchants to importers. All selling their wares with gusto.

"Pretty dress? Pretty dress for the pretty lady? We can even make it gold to match your lovely hair!"

Mari shook her head as they passed "No thank you"

"Watch it" a gruff-sounding man smoking a pipe muttered shoving past A without glancing back. A just shook his head following Trisk and Mari.

"Leather bound journals? Freshly made parchment, anyone?" Trisk was drawn to the stationary stall like a magpie attracted to anything shiny.

Mari gave him a backward glance "Trisk, don't lag behind -"

"Get your fish!" thrusted in her face was a large pink salmon "Caught fresh today. Get it while it still swims!"

She dodged the fish and seller in turn "No thank you" she said yet again "Talk about upselling" she whispered to A quickening her steps to avoid any more attempts at being sold things they either didn't need or couldn't afford. Until they passed a stall selling imported wine and other alcohols from Ryu and beyond. Mari wasn't a drinker by any means. Usually, two pints of cheap ale was enough to put her under the table. Wine she stayed well away from for obvious reasons. However, one brand they were selling caught her attention. "Wait a minute" Suddenly she put Clovis in A's arms and marched towards the stand.

"Evening, my lady. Can I interest you in any of

our products? I assure you, we only stock the finest" The seller, Pangarian like herself with mellow orange hair smiled up at her waving at the bottles on display. "I can even offer free samples if you're interested"

Mari pointed at a particular bottle. Clear glass that held a deep purple liquid. "Can I see this?" she picked it up without waiting for an answer. A wondered what all the fuss was about. It was just a bottle of wine after all. That is, until Mari exclaimed loud as anything "That bastard!"

The shout was loud enough that he almost dropped Clovis out of shock. Even the stall owner was surprised at her outburst. "What? What?"

"Pinches!" she fumed, angrily slamming the bottle back on the stall "He's selling wine. Made of those berries no doubt. He's profiting of my friends!" she then let out a long string of words so foul that would make a sailor blush in embarrassment. A was well and truly stunned for a moment, unable to say anything during her tirade. Only when she eventually ran out of steam did the stall owner manage to speak.

"So... you don't want the wine?" Mari shot him one more glare before flouncing off in a furious huff. "I'll take that as a no"

✻ ✻ ✻

Mari found a small above ground water well where she took the chance to grab a much-needed drink. Clovis padded towards her first with a small whimper. Then A appeared though he stayed a fair few feet from her. Mari met his questioning eyes and sighed. This time more resigned than angry. "Sorry about that" she said folding her arms "I just... really hate that guy"

"You said he was an Oracle?"

"No, I said he claimed to be an Oracle" she clarified "I never believed it for a moment, but you'd be amazed how many people would fall for his charms, his lies" she shook her head sighing yet again "I should have known he was up to something with those berries. Slimy git profiting off my friends..." Mari then smirked "I'm even happier I nicked his boots when I left"

A paused, looked down at his feet, and realised "No..." he gasped slowly "You did not"

Mari bit back a smile "Yeah. Don't tell anyone, but it was ridiculously easy to nab them. Idiot never locked his door" she then smiled properly "Be careful with them. Pretty sure they're made of deer hide or something"

"Wait, what?"

Whatever was about to be said was interrupted by shouting coming from around the corner. Clovis darted ahead with a bark. "Not again. Clovis!" Mari yelled darting after him. A following her as they rounded the corner. As it turned out, the shouting was coming from the very Inn they were trying to find. The bright pink painted building with vines of hanging pink flowers and white window frames was currently the setting of quite the explosive argument on the threshold. The argument was between a Pangarian man and a Bogwog.

Unlike Pangarians, Kaligans, and Borgans, Bogwogs were short stubby beings with extended limbs but walked with a hunch and barely reached the knee of the average Pangarian. They were considered unappealing to most due to their distinctive features and purple skin marred with bumps and lumps.

However, Bogwogs were known to be fabulous entertainers. They could sing a song, spin a tale, perform a dance, play and interment. The list was endless to what a Bogwog could do. That meant their skills were high in demand and high in price. Of which was apparently the cause of the argument.

"We agreed. Ten gold and no less!" the Bogwog shouted

"And I told you, no more than five!" the Innkeeper shouted back "I'm trying to make a living here"

The Bogwog retorted "And so am I. good luck finding another singer tonight. If you come to your senses and pay me what I deserve, you can find me at the tavern"

"Hey. Hey! Get back here you little – argh!" he stormed back into the Inn slamming the fuchsia pink door shut hard enough that it rattled. The Bogwog hobbled on past Mari and A with a pleased smile. Sure that the innkeeper would come crawling back soon enough. Clovis sniffed as the Bogwog passed and visibly scrunched his nose up.

"Well, that was something" commented the Half-Breed watching the Bogwog disappear down the road.

Mari had to agree, nodding in almost bemusement "At least we found the Inn. Now we just need to find Trisk and -" as if hearing he was being called upon, Trisk came walking towards the pair. Arms ladened with his newly bought writing supplies. So much so that the items were stacked up to his chin. Mari and A were both surprised and puzzled at the sheer number of writing supplies Trisk had splurged on.

"Yes, I have a problem" he stated simply

Mari blinked "You bought all that?"

"Like I said. I have a problem" he repeated "Did you find the Inn?"

"And then some. You missed one heck of an argument"

Trisk laughed "I could hear it halfway down the street" Trisk strained to look over his gathered goods to read the plaque next to the door "Talisan's all-inclusive Inn & Bar. Quality assured. Nightly entertainment, drinks half priced during happy hour... sounds like a nice place"

Mari quickly read the plaque as well and winced "Should be for the price. Two gold a head just for one night?" at her feet, Clovis was taking a moment to nibble at an itchy spot on his leg when a sound caught his attention. His ears perked up at the noise. Out from the shadows slinked a cat with silky white fur coat with bright yellow eyes and a bell around its collar.

Clovis being a puppy, immediately jumped after

the animal to play. The cat screeched and bolted away in defence causing Clovis to chase even harder.

"Oh, for crying out loud" A sighed in exasperation "Clovis, get back here!" like before, Mari hurried after the puppy calling his name. A turned to Trisk. "Get us a room. We'll be right back" he then added to the chase by following Mari. The dog was slowly growing on him but right now he was reminded why he hadn't liked dogs in the first place.

Trisk shouted after him "Good luck!" before making his way to the Inn.

The bell above the door jungled as he entered through the door. Despite the outside being pink, the interior was a light blue with purple and red accents. Dark mahogany furniture and old portraits of unknown people decorated the entrance quite nicely. Trisk followed the sounds of laughter and chatter where he found the bar area of the Inn. The large open space took up most of the ground floor of the building. It was filled almost to the brim with people at the bar itself and sat at the tables littered around the red painted room. He could see a small stage on the other side of the room that was currently unoccupied.

He passed on until he managed to locate the check in desk where the Innkeeper Talisan was sat with his head in his hands groaning. "Um, hello?"

"What?" the other man snapped "Sorry. Been a long day. How can I help you?

Trisk set the pile down on the floor next to his feet "I'd like to book a room for tonight. Three people"

"Sorry mate. All sold out. Only got one room available and that's for the singer tonight" he explained with annoyance dripping from his voice "Who just tried to overcharge me for his frankly lacklustre singing voice. Bogwogs for you"

Trisk nodded "I see. Anything I could help with"

Talisan snorted "My friend, unless you can pull a singer out of your pocket for tonight, I'd rather you didn't" he sighed

The Scan's eyes widened as an idea formed in his head "Actually, now that you mention it..."

"No" Mari later stated when Trisk told her of his plan.

"Why not? It's a great plan! You sing and we get a free room for the night. Free!" he emphasised "I don't see the problem"

Her eyes went wide with indignation "You didn't ask my permission first! And who says I can even sing?"

"We've heard you singing all the time" A commented looking confused

"Humming is a lot different to full-blown singing. I might not even be that good"

"Don't be ridiculous!" Trisk said with wide open arms "I'm sure you'll do great. Besides, it's only a few songs. Even if you are bad, the innkeeper and I have already made our agreement. Just give it a try. What's the worst that can happen?" Trisk then grabbed Mari by the arm and started pulling her to the building.

"Hey, hey, hey! Trisk! I made no agreement to this. Let me go!" Mari fumed trying in vain to break free of the Scan's surprisingly firm grip around her wrist.

Lagging behind, A picked Clovis up in his arms once more "You think if I leave now, they'll notice I'm gone?"

Clovis barked.

"Yeah, I didn't think so" A sighed then followed the pair into the Inn

❈ ❈ ❈

"Apologies for the wait, ladies and gentlemen and everything in between" Talisan announced to the awaiting crowd in the bar. "Please welcome to the stage tonight, Miss Mari" The waiting guests young and old, wealthy and poor, drunk and sober alike, all applauded politely as Mari awkwardly took the stage. At one of the tables sat A and Trisk with Clovis perched on the table between them.

A continued to keep his hood up as to not cause another incident like what happened in Riven. "She looks nervous" Trisk whispered to A in concern

"She looks like she might be sick" the Half-Breed corrected

Talisan snapped his fingers, and the house band began to play. The tune was upbeat and joyful, one that was composed to get one's feet tapping with the beat. The band consisted of string and wind instruments with the lute player being the most prominent. Mari glanced over to them, waiting her queue. Swallowing back her ever-increasing nerves, she started to sing.

In a land of ancient lore, where heroes bold do roam,

A tale unfolds, untold before, to make the heart a home,

Come gather 'round, both young and old, and heed this humble bard,

For I shall sing a tale untold, beneath the moon's

regard.

"...Wow" Trisk gasped at the utterly dazzling voice Mari possessed. He wasn't the only one as almost everyone in the bar had their sole attention on Mari. Cheering her on and clapping in tune with the music. Mari smiled almost in disbelief people genuinely liked her singing.

Oh… hear this call, this journey's song,
Where brave souls rise and right the wrong.
Through trials dire, and battles fierce,
They'll find their strength, their purpose clear.

"Go Mari!" Trisk cheered while Clovis barked above the music

A maiden fair with eyes of light, and spirit pure and true,
A Knight of armour shining bright, a loved one to peruse.
They set forth on a fateful night, their destinies entwined,

To face the dark, embrace the light, and leave no foe behind.

Oh... hear this call, this journey's song,
Where brave souls rise and right the wrong.
Through trials dire, and battles fierce,
They'll find their strength, their purpose clear.

A suddenly hit Trisk on the shoulder to grab his attention. When Trisk looked at him, A gestured to the crowd pointing out that they were so impressed with Mari's talent as a singer that they were literally throwing money at her. Trisk nodded understanding what he meant. Using empty flagons that once held their ale, Trisk and A went about the crowd holding out the flagons to collect the coins.

Through misty woods and mountains tall, they'll brave the tempest's ire,

And answer comrade's desperate call, to kindle freedom's fire.

Their courage, love, a beacon strong, shall guide them through the dark,

For in their hearts, the song of hope, will light the

sacred spark.

"Everybody!" Mari cheered waving with swooping hand gestures to the crowd. Emboldened by her singing and with joy in their hearts, the crowd joined her in singing the next chorus. Trisk and A were well on their way to filling up their flagons with coins. Trisk happily joined in with the chorus as well and A, despite everything about his personality stating otherwise, joined in as well but nowhere near as loud as Trisk was.

Oh... hear this call, this journey's song,
Where brave souls rise and right the wrong.
Through trials dire, and battles fierce,
They'll find their strength, their purpose clear.

Mari all but laughed in delight. Her beaming smile was glowing as much as her hair was in the candlelight.

So here we stand, in rapture's thrall, as this performance ends,
But in our hearts, we'll hear the call, this tale forever lends.

So raise your voices, let them ring! And let the music play,

For in this ballad, let us sing... and greet the light of day!

***

As fate would have it, A and his group avoided running into Urdel's company by only a few hours. Desmond watched from the sidelines, chest squeezing with discomfort as the caravan burnt down before them. The man named Cassadore had begged them to leave his home alone, pleading that there were dangerous items inside that could be devastating if released. Urdel hadn't listened. As soon as he found out the Half-Breed had passed through these parts and Cassadore had let him go without issue, Urdel had seen red and ordered for the caravan to be destroyed.

Said owner of the caravan was lying flat on his back on the grass with a head wound. "Please... you don't know what you're doing" he managed to slur out in between bouts of horrific agony ripping through his skull.

Urdel smirked as he walked towards the small pile of items his men had taken before they set the fire. He's allowed them to take whatever they fancied before setting the flames. Desmond had stayed well away unable to meet anyone's eye. Disgusted at what Urdel was doing. His thoughts returned yet again to Rei who he hoped had made it back alright. "Quite the collection you had" the Borgan mused, picking up a tempered glass bottle with almost childlike curiosity, "How on earth did you capture a cloud?"

Cassadore tried to get up but realised he couldn't. The pain in his head so searing with every movement it left him paralysed where he lay. "Please... Don't - Don't touch that"

"Or what?" he retorted violently shaking the bottle in his giant hand. The cloud inside already shifting into a raging storm "What can a little rain cloud do?" he looked down at the bottle with a shrug "Well... Since you asked so nicely" he set the bottle down on the ground much to Cassadore's relief. Desmond wondered just what was in that jar to cause such panic.

Then Urdel shattered the glass by stomping his heavy foot down upon it. His Borgan weight was easily able to break even tempered glass. Cassadore's cry of "NO!" went unheard as Urdel and everyone else was thrown off their feet as the storm took to the sky. Urdel howled in pain as the force of the storm had injured his leg from ankle to knee. The star-studded sky instantly began to darken and rumble with ominous thunder. The now black as void night flashed with streaks of lightning forking into the ground where guardsmen narrowly avoided being struck.

"What in the world...?" Urdel whispered looking upwards. The flashes of lightning showed the swirling clouds raging uninhibited since the day Cassadore had captured it.

Cassadore stared helplessly up at the sky, a lone tear falling from his face that was soon washed away by an intense downpour of freezing rain and hail.

"What have you done?"

"Captain! We should get going!" Desmond yelled over the now howling wind

Urdel nodded and began ordering his men to begin marching onwards. His back turned; Desmond failed to see the lightning illuminate the figure standing next to the now smouldering caravan. His eyes empty. His body broken. Bright red blood coating his once pristine guardsmen uniform. Another flash and he was gone, and the storm above began to shift. Desmond glanced behind him, eyes squinting through the rain so sure he had sensed something.

"Desmond! Let's go!"

"Coming Captain"

CHAPTER THIRTEEN

Race to Marden

Bringing his horse to a stop, Yuen let out a harsh groan of pain. One arm moved to wrap around his middle as a searing pain ripped through him. He hadn't rested since leaving TeraKyla. So focused on getting to Marden before Urdel could he had forgone any rest at all. Only stopping to let his horse catch his breath and eat when needed. Yuen pulled out the Bluebird milk but caught sight of his horse before he could drink it. If Yuen didn't know any better, he'd swear the horse was judging him.

"Oh, come on, really?" he sighed noticing his horse was focused on the Bluebird milk in his hand "It's not like that. I'm in pain" his horse let out a nicker of judgement. Yuen glanced at the bottle and sighed, putting it back in his bag "There. Happy ya big lug?" he winced again at the pain but managed not to reach for the milk again. Lest he be judged by his horse of all things.

He gave Ferin a pat on the neck just underneath his well-maintained mane. "You know, you're lucky your cute or I wouldn't put up with this nonsense"

His thoughts on his injury quickly faded when a loud rumble above his head caught his attention. The hair on the back on his head stood on end at the volume. Looking upwards his eyes widened slightly as he witnessed the clouds get almost dragged out of sight by the force of the sudden wind. The wind swiftly turned to a howling gust that almost blew his cloak right off his person. His eyes followed the quickly moving clouds and felt a twinge of fear he hadn't felt to such a degree for many a year. In the distance, admits the darkening sky and growing clouds, a great storm was brewing on the horizon. It was then he was hit with a downpour of freezing rain.

Yuen hung his head letting the rain fall upon him Well, isn't that just peachy?" he sighed shaking his head "In pain, behind schedule, and now it's bloody raining..." Yuen muttered turning back to Ferin. He was about to hoist himself back onto the saddle when he heard a moan on the wind. One filled with pain that made him pause. Ferin too heard it and turned his head to face the path.

"It's always something... Hello?" Yuen called

"Help me..." came the moaning voice again with a plead

Yuen remained suspicious. He unsheathed his sword and slowly stepped forward. The first thing he spotted through the pouring rain was the smouldering remains of a caravan. The fire he could tell had been recent by the smoke and steam still filtering into the sky. Yuen's eyes scanned the area till his eyes fell upon the injured man lying on the grass near the caravan. He sheathed his sword and hurried over to the man.

"Sir?" He asked the fallen Kaligan

Cassador's pale eyes fluttered open only to shut tight yet again "Please, you... You have to warn them"

"Hang on. Let me help you first" Yuen whistled for Ferin. On his horse was his medical kit. Members of both the Guard and Garrison were trained in basic healing for on and off the battlefield. So Yuen could at least bandage the head wound Cassadore was sporting. He helped the Kaligan rest with his back against a tree. The rain made applying the white fabric redundant but at least Yuen could say he tried. He fished out the bottle of Bluebird milk. Hesitating for a split second, he offered the bottle to Cassadore. "Here. You need this more than I do"

Cassadore gulped the bottle down, a little dribbling down his chin "Thank you" he said afterwards. Cassadore looked at him "You're not one of them are you?"

The Guard shook his head "I don't think so. One of who?"

"Those Garrison. Lead by that brutish Brogan"

he sneered blinking away the raindrops on his eyelashes.

Yuen felt his stomach drop "Urdel? You – you've met Urdel?"

"Kind of hard to avoid someone that size" he managed to joke then wince "Urgh, my head…"

Yuen was confused. Surely he had been ahead of Urdel when he began following A and his comrades. He had sent word back after all. "Are you sure it was him? Maybe it was another Borgan you met"

Cassadore gave him a withered look "Know many Borgans in charge of a Garrison squad decked in armour"

"Yeah, that's - that's definitely Urdel" the Guard muttered rubbing his eyes and feeling dreed creep up his spine. He pushed that feeling down for now. The man before him needed medical attention he couldn't provide "Come on. I'll get you to Elayas. There must be a doctor there for you-"

Cassadore shook his aching head pushing away Yuen's arm "No time. You must hurry. Warn them of what is to come" his grey eyes shone bright with emotion, pleading Yuen to heed to his begging "If not, they won't have time to escape"

"Escape what? Urdal? The Garrison? Who?"

The Kaligan sighed despondent his gaze now fixed on the churning storm above. The rain now hammering in strength. "The storm. They'll never escape the storm..."

Yuen had no idea what that meant. He looked up as well but didn't understand why some bad weather was such a threat. "I don't understand. It's just rain" he said hoping that would ease the older man's worries.

Instead, it earned him a glare filled with fire and a hard shove to the chest. Which didn't help his injury in the slightest. "Don't you get it? We are on the brink of catastrophe! Urdel released a monster into the world. One that will destroy anything in its wake when it reaches full strength. This storm? This is only the beginning"

The rumble of thunder made both men turn

their heads up to the sky. The dark grey clouds were moving once more. Yuen stood up grimacing to gain a better perspective. Now that he thought about it, he had never seen a storm appear out of the blue like this before. Nor had he ever seen one grow so strong so quickly. Suddenly, he was somewhat worried that the Kaligan may not be speaking madness after all. "It's heading north" he announced "it's heading to..." lightning flashed, and Yuen gulped. Within the storm high above he spotted, just for a moment, the shadowy figure of a person. "Oh Gods..." he looked back to Cassadore "What is that thing?"

"That, my boy, is death" he answered resting his head back onto the three "There's nothing that can be done. Anything in its path will be nothing but rubble"

Yuen shook his head defiantly "There are people there. People who – they'll be killed!"

"You think I don't know that?" Cassadore said forcing himself to stand up using the tree for support. "You think I'm not acutely aware of what will happen. I begged him not to let that thing out, but he did so without hesitation. And for what?" he asked anger fuelling him. By then the winds where they stood had calmed slightly as the storm was continuing its slow ascent north. "There's nothing that can be done to stop it. All that can be done is warn he people. Have them take shelter while they still can"

Yuen's stomach churned at the ominous warning. He could scarcely believe such a threat existed or that it was powerful enough to control the weather itself. The Guard, who had faced bloodshed, destruction, and war, was powerless against such a creature. Still, he shook his head defiantly. If there was one thing he'd learned over the years; it was that no matter how impossible the odds, a solution was somewhere to be found. He marched over to Cassadore grabbing him by the collar of his soaking shirt. "Come on" he ordered dragging him towards his horse Ferin.

Hoof steps pounded the path as thunder once

again rumbled above. Yuen whipped the reigns to make Ferin go faster, Cassadore sat behind him hanging on limply. Every galloping stride was like a knife to his side, but Yuen powered through.

The doors to Talisan's Inn blew open startling the patrons and guests. Water dripped onto the wooden floor as Yuen helped carry Cassadore in with the Kaligan's arm over his shoulder. Blood staining his short from where his stiches had broken "We need a doctor over here!"

❋ ❋ ❋

"Rain, rain go away. Come again another day" Mari sang quietly, sighing in disappointment that the horrible weather refused to let up. They had been surprised at how sudden the storm had appeared but with an ever-approaching deadline it wasn't possible to wait out the foul weather. So all three sat on their horses who trudged along through the wind and rain and the surprisingly freezing temperature. Clovis settled himself in A's pack protected from the rain.

On her left, Trisk mumbled to himself as he counted the profits Mari made at the Inn "Ninety-one, ninety-two, ninety-three..."

Ahead of Mari and Trisk, A glanced back at them. With all three how wearing hooded cloaks to shield from the rain, A no longer stood out as such. "You didn't think a children's song would actually work, did you?"

"One can live in hope" she responded stroking the wet mane of her horse "Don't worry. We'll be there soon"

Trisk finished counting and placed everything back in his bag with a satisfied grin. He now had two bags in his possession. His original which he had taken with him when he left the Redencon Library. The other on his back was bought in Elayas to hold all his new stationary. "Final count. Thirty-eight coppers. Sixty-five silvers. And a hundred and thirteen gold coins. You made more than Urdel's down payment"

Mari choked a gasp "Are you serious?"

"Congrats" A spoke and that's all he said to her on the matter.

"Wow..." she breathed "I've never made that much before in my life" The rumbling thunder above quickly dampened her mood once more "Is it me, or is this storm getting worse?"

Trisk nodded already sick of being so wet "Definitely getting worse. I will be very happy when we get to Marden. Hopefully there I can ring out my socks. A? How's Clovis doing?"

"Currently snoring. Pup can sleep through a hurricane, I swear" the Half-Breed answered. That's when the trio passed a marble stone sign embedded into the ground. The words 'Welcome to Marden' embossed with blue coloured stone in contrast to the white marble.

Mari groaned in relief "Finally"

"Hey, A? Quick question" Trisk spoke

A shook his head almost instantly "I thought I told you, no personal questions"

"I know, it's just – if you can't read or write, I'm curious to know how you know your way around Endonia"

The singer of the group made a gesture of silence with sharp eyes, hoping Trisk would get the message to stop talking. A brought Firefoot to a stop and the other two did the same. He turned his head to look at Trisk "I've never been able to stay in one spot for long. You travel long enough; you get to learn the names of things through word of mouth. It also helps to know your right from your left" he then kicked his horse into gear and off he trotted on ahead.

Trisk blinked "Was that a joke?"

Mari shrugged "I think so?"

Marden was situated within the mountain scape of North Endonia. The city trailed upwards from the gates to the grand marble Monastery built into the face of the mountain itself. The Brotherhood of Astrid was the jewel of the city. Its holy order members celebrated as the link between Endonia and the Four Gods they followed with Astrid being the collective name for the Four.

Though that day the Monastery was engulfed in a fog mist that was mixed with pounding rain and howling winds. Though the weather was nothing short of horrendous with the storm continuing to build and grow and churn, there was no shortage of people on the streets. As the trio found the stable and settled their horses in from the bad weather, they noticed a large gathering start to form near the jailhouse of the city.

Passing by was a child with his family pulling his parents by the wrists "Come on! We're gonna miss the beheading!" he said urging them to hurry up

Trisk became concerned "Beheading?" he voiced feeling a little sick "I thought executions were only done in the Capital"

"Maybe the guy's too dangerous to transport?" Mari shrugged, gripping her cloak so it didn't fly off "By the Four, this weather is horrible!"

A ensured Clovis was secure in his pack before speaking "Let's go. We're running behind as it is"

Like Ryu, Marden was built in three sections only unlike the towering multi-class city, all of Marden was equal in wealth and status. No one was above one another, something that the Brotherhood had made real thanks to their tireless efforts to promote peace and respect to all. Aside from the city's official buildings, the grand Monastery which was topped with red singled roofs and billowing flags, no house stood apart from one another.

To get to the Monastery, the trio had to climb up the countless connecting staircases also made of white marble. The rain made the steps perilous, so the climb was a slow one. Both Mari and Trisk losing their footing on more than one occasion. Saved only by A's quick reflexes. They had to pass the jailhouse to keep going but Trisk found herself drawn to the growing crowd who were eagerly awaiting the spilling of blood. Mari and A joined him after noticing he had fallen behind.

In the centre of the jeering crowd was the executioner's block. They witnessed a young Pangarian man of rich violet hair being led to the chopping block where the axe man's blade awaited him. Surprisingly, the man sowed no fear or anger on his face. Instead, he wore a look of peace. As if he had been awaiting this moment for quite some time. Even through the pouring pain, it was clear that he was unfazed by the prospect of his death.

"I wonder what he did" Trisk murmured

Held back by two armoured guards, another man dressed in finery struggled against their hold on him. He was a Kaligan like Trisk. His white hair was tied into an intricate braid soaked by the rain and held up by a golden circlet. At first glance, it was obvious he was a member of Nobility. "Forgive me, my dear Tharian!" the man pleaded, his dears washed away by the rain "By the Gods above, forgive me!"

Tharian simply smiled at him "There is nothing to forgive. I die for you with peace in my soul. May we meet again, my Prince"

His head was forced onto the block by the masked executioner. The prince desperately tried to look away, but the guards held his face in place. Keeping him facing towards the execution. He screamed. The axe rose. But mercifully, the Prince fainted before the blade could meet the neck of his dear Tharian. He slumped against the two guards in a dead faint. The crowd audibly gasped as the Pangarian's severed head hit the ground with a squelching thud.

Mari turned her head away before the blade fell, closing her eyes and shaking her head in sympathy for the Kaligan prince. The prince was then carried back into the jailhouse and the crowd dispersed. The people of Marden returned to their daily lives while the body of Tharian was taken away.

Even A appeared disturbed at what they had seen "Poor sod" he commented before leaving the area. Mari followed suit but Trisk remained for a few moments longer. For some reason, his grey eyes lingered on the unconscious prince and the rough way the guards were carrying him inside. "Trisk!" A shouted shaking him from his thoughts

"Y-yeah, coming..."

* * *

"So... Many... Stairs..." panted Mari pausing to catch her breath

Trisk couldn't help but agree wholeheartedly as he too stopped just behind her, chest heaving from the exhaustion "And here I thought Ryu had too many staircases" he said while gripping the handrail so not to fall. "How much further?"

A craned his neck to peer upwards, squinting as rain pelted his face. He could just about make out the shadow of the Monastery peeking through the fog, from his point of view it could eclipse the mountain with its commanding presence. "Can't be much further" inside his bag, Clovis peaked his head out. He sniffed the air for a moment, sneezed, and then promptly curled back inside out of the rain.

"Let's keep going" A instructed, gesturing them to continue.

The Scan reached out his hand, finding he could barely see past where his hand could reach. "It's as thick as soup up here. And still no end to this Gods forsaken rain"

"I don't care what you two say, I am not leaving this place until the storm passes" declared Mari catching up to her comrades. At last, the trio found their way to the grand doors of the Monastery. The doors themselves were three times the size of A who was the tallest of the group. Made of deep dark Castilian wood with large golden rappers decorated with the embodiment of a soaring bird.

A grabbed one of the rappers and knocked on the door thrice. The three knocks rung loudly with each hit against the wood. The door opened after a brief moment of waiting. At the door was a Pangarian man with curled berry blue hair and a decorative piercing on his right rounded ear. Along with that, he wore simple brown robes with a sash of brightly coloured fabric around his waist. He took one look at them and stepped aside to let them in. "Please, come in. All are welcome to seek refuge at our humble house"

"Thank you" Trisk said on behalf of all of them, taking the lead to get out of the storm. Mari stepped in next and A last.

The Pangarian closed the door with a firm shove. Trisk and Mari shed their soaking cloaks and hung them on the offered hooks by the door. A hose to keep his on despite the water that was dripping off him as to hide his heritage. "How may I help you?" the Brother asked curiously "I'm afraid you're a tad early for midday blessing"

"We were hoping to speak to a member of your Brotherhood" Trisk explained "He's a Borgan named Rylon"

The man nodded with a hum of acknowledgement "Yes. Brother Rylon. Hard fellow to ignore. If you would like to follow me" he gestured them to follow him "And please, bring the dog" he smiled to Clovis who was now sat by Mari's legs panting as if he had climbed the steps himself and not been carried up them. "He's a sucker for a cute animal"

At the gates of Marden, Urdel glared up at the fog-covered Monastery. Of all the places in Endonia for his brother to hide out, it still puzzled him why he chose here of all places. Desmond ran up to him. "Sighting confirmed, Captain" he informed "Three travellers matching their descriptions were last seen heading upwards"

Urdel's glare shifted to a twisted smirk "Excellent. Let's go"

Pushing his horse as fast as the animal was able to go, Yuen prayed he'd reach Marden in time.

CHAPTER FOURTEEN

Raging Storm

The interior of the Marden Monastery was made of the darkest black marble. Perfectly structured walls met the cold rock of the mountain face. The walls though black glowed almost gold thanks to the countless ever-burning candles that lined the isle and adorned the walls in gold-encrusted holders. Somewhere in the building, harmonious deep voices rang out as they sang hymns dedicated to the Four Gods they worshipped.

The Four Gods represented the Four Pilers of their belief. As they were led further inside, A was the first to spot Rylon close to the altar of the main hall. Walking closer they could hear him reciting a prayer while kneeling before the overshadowing statue that represented the Four. Four heads adorning one body with its arms spread wide to welcome all into their embrace.

"...And it by the will of man that we humble ourselves before you" Rylon spoke, his voice similar to his brother's but softer "Father, show me courage. Mother, grant me wisdom. Elder, give me strength. Child, teach me love. These are the blessings you give and the lessons we must learn. By the Four, protect us"

The Pangarian Brother made a noise to gain his attention "Ahem. Brother Rylon? You have visitors"

The Borgan stood from his kneeling position with a grunt. At full height, he made for quite the foreboding figure. Till he turned to face them and the differences between him and Urdel were clear as day. Rylon's eyes were gentle whereas Urdel's were sharp. His beard while also impressive, Rylon left it grow free down to his stomach. "Welcome" he greeted with a nod of his head "I am Brother Rylon. How may I be of service?" he glanced down and spotted Clovis. The squeak of excitement that escaped him was surprisingly adorable for someone his size "Oh, look at you, you bonnie little thing! May I?"

"Um, by all means" Trisk said, and Rylon eagerly picked the puppy up into his oversized arms that bulged against the simple robes.

Rylon laughed "Apologies. I just simply adore animals. Especially puppies such as this little guy" Clovis didn't seem to mind the stranger holding him. He was just satisfied with getting more attention. "So, what can I help you with? I don't recognise you from Marden, so I take it you are travellers?"

Outside citizens of Marden still out in the horrific weather were pushed aside with no care at all. Dozens of footsteps pounded the marble staircase up towards the Monastery. At the head was Urdel who was practically brimming with anticipation for what was to come. Just behind him, Desmond felt his stomach sink with a wave of sudden anxiety the closer they got to the grand building.

Not far behind was Yuen who all but fell off his horse in the rush to dismount his horse, almost crying out in agony as pain ripped through him once more. But he had no time to focus on his pain. He was running out of time.

Unbeknownst to the panicked Yuen, Urdel's reinforcements were only a few miles behind. Five hundred men strong, all Pangarian men donned in shining armour forged of iron. At the helm, a man of great power, great influence, and most of all, an all-consuming need for revenge. Lord Callum.

Back inside, A spoke "We were asked to come find you on behalf of your brother. The name Urdel sound familiar?" almost instantly, the cheerful demeanour fell to that of confusion.

"Urdel?" he breathed a single small laugh "I haven't heard from him in years. Didn't think I ever would after our last altercation" he bent down to set Clovis back on the floor, puppy whining with displeasure.

Trisk continued "He told us that you were once a criminal. Is that true?"

"Wait, what now?" Mari questioned with a frown

The Borgan let out a weary sigh "It is not something I'm proud of. I made a lot of mistakes in my life. Many I deeply regret"

Coming back into the hall, the Pangarian Brother from earlier spoke up "We found Brother Rylon injured on the outskirts of Marden. His men had abandoned him, so he was brought here for aid"

"Took my vows that same month" Rylon added with a proud smile "These good people saved me when the world turned against me. I owed them that much at least. Though I must ask, why did Urdel send you to find me? The last time we spoke he vowed to kill me on sight if he were to ever see me again" he said it as if it were a joke but a flash of pain in his dark green eyes proved otherwise.

Once again, Trisk took the initiative "It's about your father. He's dying and Urdel wants you to come back to Riven to see him before he goes"

Outside the dark wooden doors, Urdel gave the signal for his men to hold position. He ever so gently pulled the door open just enough that he could peer inside.

Rylon tilted his head, brow furrowed in bewilderment "My Father?" he repeated in a tone that emphasised his confusion "My father died years ago. Died of Endon Flu when Urdel and I were teenagers"

"What?" Mari questioned glancing to Trisk "But, I thought you said -"

"A..." the Scan whispered pale as a ghost "I think we were tricked"

A pinched the bridge of his nose "Oh, you think?"

The doors to the Monastery flew open. Dozens of men marched inside with their swords at the ready, the rain and wind following them like a desperate animal. "Forgive the interruption," Urdel announced pulling down his hood to reveal himself

"But I simply love to make an entrance" the doors were firmly shut by his Garrison. Brotherhood members who had come when they heard the commotion quickly retreated when they caught sight of the swords.

"Urdel" Rylon spoke, his voice now sounding tired "I wish you had told me you were coming. I'd have prepared refreshments"

Urdel walked forward, cloak billowing as he did so "Always with the sarcasm, dear brother. I'm amazed no one has cut out your tongue for it yet"

Sensing the growing unease of her comrades, Mari whispered, "That's Urdel?"

Trisk nodded "That's the guy who paid us to find Rylon" he responded back in a quiet voice "But - but I don't understand why he's here"

"It was a trap" A spoke, louder so to catch the two Borgan's attention "This was all some plot to catch your brother unarmed, wasn't it?"

Urdel shook his head whilst chuckling "You're only half right. You see, my brother's untimely demise was just a bonus. Collateral damage, as it were" The Captain then turned his gaze from his brother to A, eyes ablaze with a devilish excitement "The truth is, I needed you here. In this exact spot. At this exact time"

Both Mari and Trisk glanced to A, but the Half-Breed remained stoic where he stood. "And why is that?" A asked lightly, on hand slowly reaching for one of his knives.

"Lord Callum sends his regards" Urdel told him and just like that, A became a statue. Trisk saw the colour drain from the Half-Breed's face. Saw A's eyes widen, and the light blue irises shrink to pinpoints. Even the prospect of facing of a horde of Bandits hadn't spooked A. but whoever this Lord Callum was, he put the fear of the Gods in him. Trisk aslo felt a twinge of recognition at the name, sure he had heard it somewhere before.

Trisk took a step forward "Who is Lord Callum?"

"Oh for – Do not tell me you're involved with that mad man" Rylon voiced with clear distain

"Even I wasn't dumb enough to break bread with him. Are you insane?"

Urdel rolled his eyes "Choice words coming from a criminal"

"I left that life behind" sneered Rylon "You knew that. Father knew that. I wonder what he'd think seeing his golden boy act like such a backstabbing degenerate"

The other brother's nostrils flared "Oh, you substandard little -"

"Lord Callum! Who is he? What does he have to do with this?" Mari shouted cutting through the argument like a knife would cut through flesh.

Urdel glinted her way, finding it hilarious that A was still frozen in place "He's a nobleman from Osjorn. He made his fortune through trading, exports, and mining" the Borgan clarified "Your 'friend' over there used to work for Lord Callum in the mines of the Hathbert Coast. Not a lot of employment opportunities for a Half-Breed, as you can guess"

"So? What does he have to do with the Half-Breed?" Rylon demanded growing tired of his brother's showmanship.

"The Half-Breed..." he paused giving A the darkest smile he could muster "Is responsible for the death of Lord Callum's youngest son, Tyrmir. That man, that freak of nature, is a murderer"

Slowly, Mari and Trisk turned to A "A? What is he talking about?"

Finally, the Half-Breed regained the ability to speak, glaring at Urdel with fire in his soul "It was an accident" he muttered "I never wanted to hurt him. I just – I just wanted to know why those men had to die down in the dark when they could have been saved" feeling a surge of fury overcome him, A pulled out both his knives and held one in each shaking hand "Tell me, good captain," he said dripping with sarcasm "Did good old Lord Callum tell you why he left us to rot down in that mine? Did he tell you how long those men screamed for help until they died? Did he!?"A would have lunged for the Borgan had not Trisk and Mari grabbed him by the arms holding him back from doing something he would later regret "Let me go!"

"I don't know why I expected a civilised conversation with a Half-Breed" Urdel then snapped his fingers "Clap him in irons. Lord Callum will be here soon enough"

The shift from righteous fury to pure panic was instantaneous. A had nightmares for years of what would happen to him if Lord Callum should ever find him, and now they were all coming true. Now instead of struggling to break free so he could attack Urdel, he became paralysed as the Garrison began to come closer.

Out of nowhere, Rylon stepped between the trio and the dozens of armed men "This is a house of worship. By order of the Brotherhood of Astrid, I demand you leave this place. These three are under our protection" at his feet, Clovis growled threateningly, teeth bared and body low ready to pounce. The garrison soldiers hesitated. Their orders were already dubious enough, but no one was brave enough or stupid enough to defy a member of the Brotherhood.

Urdel let out a swear "For the love of – You cannot protect them. This Brotherhood of yours means shit to me. I will have that Half-Breed even if I have to slaughter you all myself to do it!" Urdel made his point clear by unsheathing his Greatsword. The weapon was a thing of beauty if the situation hadn't made the almost glowing blade terrifying in its use. "Tell you what. I'll bring Lord Callum your head and charge extra for bringing you back quiet"

"Captain, maybe we should -"

"Shut. Up" the Borgan warned Desmond "If you think you're safe because I took pity on you, then you're more foolish than that idiot Rei"

Desmond's stomach dropped "Rei...? What about -" The truth dawned on him in that very moment "... Rei never turned back to Riven, did he?"

The Borgan laughed cruelly "Look at that. I suppose there is a brain in that head of yours"

Desmond didn't hesitate. Unlike A, no one held him back from charging at Urdel. However, Urdel simply socked him with his massive fist and Desmond crumpled to the floor. "Anyone else want to go against their commanding officer?" he asked the remaining Garrison. No one said a word "That's what I thought"

Urdel took a single step forward, the sword glinting in the candlelight threateningly when the doors to the Monastery flew open once more. In staggered Yuen soaked to the bone but with his sword in hand and gasping for breath. "We need to get out of here!" he shouted, his voice echoing throughout the grand hall.

"What the – Guard?" A said in disbelief

"Ah, Guard Delson. To what do I owe the pleasure?" Urdel asked as if he wasn't about to commit multiple murders just moments ago.

Yuen hobbled forward, face twisting in pain with every step. "Urdel, you mad bastard. You've doomed us all" he then pointed behind him to the open doors. Marden had all been engulfed in the storm with how much strength it now possessed. It was astonishing Yuen found his way up to them at all "That storm is your doing. You caused this!"

For a moment, Urdel was perplexed "Excuse me?"

"That caravan you raided. You let loose a sentient storm" Yuen pressed further sounding desperate "You've let loose a bloody Galomorick!!"

Trisk went weak at the knees and had to be supported by Mari and A "Gods no..." he gasped "Cassadore, he... oh Gods" his reaction made the other Garrison men, especially Desmond, a reason to pause.

One piped up "Galoma - what? What the hell is a -"

That's when the Monastery, which was built to withstand anything nature could throw at it, began to shake. It threw men off their feet. The heavy wooden doors came flying off from the strength of the wind. The intricately designed stained glass windows shattered all at once as the wind itself howled like a wild beast. The Galomorick Storm had reached its full power.

The wind extinguished the candles engulfing the hall in darkness, only the shunted daylight giving any form of light. The building continued to rumble and shake. It was as if the mountain itself was shuddering under the strength of the storm. One could only imagine what the city was experiencing at that same moment.

The wind extinguished the candles engulfing the hall in darkness, only the shunted daylight giving any form of light. The building continued to rumble and shake. It was as if the mountain itself was trembling under the strength of the storm. One could only imagine what the city was experiencing at that same moment.

One of the marble pillars cracked and began to topple to the floor. "Move!" Mari screamed as she, Trisk, and A barely jumped out of the way in time. The trio landed on the tiled floor with a thud, Clovis chasing after them. They pressed themselves against the wall in the corner watching as the Monastery crumble around them. Fixtures hundreds of years old fell apart like they were made or paper and not ancient stone. Clovis leapt into Trisk's arms whimpering in fear.

"What do we do?" A asked eyes darting around "Trisk, what do we do?" he repeated when Trisk didn't answer.

"There's nothing we can do!" the Kaligan cried "We're all going to die!"

Mari could only laugh in disbelief "This is what I get for leaving the forest!"

After narrowly avoiding being crushed by falling rocks, Yuen skidded towards the trio "Are you three alright?!" he shouted barely able to hear over the raging winds.

"Define alright!?" Mari shouted back her golden hair flying wildly "I hope you have a plan!"

Yuen scanned the area and spotted a door on the opposite side of the hall. The door had remained shut despite everything, so he could only hope that meant it was secure "There!"

"I hope you're right about this!" A yelled taking the offered arm. That's when the exposed roof of the grand hall couldn't withstand the raging, unrelenting storm any longer. Slowly and then all at once the roof came away exposing all inside to the utter devastation that was to come. Above them, the Galomorick had taken the form of a tornado. The largest any of them had ever seen.

Its twisting winds had already caused incredible destruction. Pieces of buildings, animals, and poor people had been swept into the unrelenting winds, their voices screaming out for help that would never come. At the heart of it all a single figure remained doned in shadow but his presence was somehow more terrifying than the storm itself.

That figure was the Glaromorick's heart.

CHAPTER FIFTEEN

Monster in the Sky

"HANG ON TO SOMETHING!" Rylon bellowed "Anything nailed down, quick!"

Desperate panic ensued as everyone ran like headless hens to find something that could hold them to the floor. Two Garrison officers shrieked when they were caught in the wind, arms and legs flaying wildly as they were sucked upwards to the sky. Bolts of lightning struck the floor of the Monastery, some of Urdel's men getting struck as they ran. Trisk clung onto one of the remaining pillars that had yet to collapse. Mari hid under one of the pews that managed to stay in place. A had the wild idea of using the ropes of the drapery as a makeshift harness around his waist.

Terrified screams engulfed what remained of the grand hall. Out of the corner of his eye, Trisk spotted Clovis being sucked up into the storm. The dog howled as he was lifted off the ground "Clovis!" he panicked, letting go of the pillar to catch the puppy before it was too late. That left Trisk vulnerable and the Galomorick would spare no one. "No, no, no!" he gasped as his feet began to lift off the ground. He instinctively threw Clovis to the floor to save him but was too far away to grab anything himself "Help me!"

Out of nowhere, A appeared grabbing both his legs firmly. His actions saved Trisk only for a moment, For A too became a victim of the storm. "Hang on!" he instructed Trick when they both were being sucked into the storm. The drapery rope went taught but that salvation lasted mere seconds. The rope snapped.

Mari bolted from her hiding spot and grabbed the rope in the nick of time. She gripped the rope with all her strength, her feet sliding against the floor. "I got you!" she promised "I got you!" but as she was lifted off the ground as well, she knew her efforts were in vain.

By the skin of his teeth, Yuen reached her in time. He grasped her ankles and held on tight, trying his hardest to pull the three of them back to the ground. Ignoring how his injury was screaming at him to stop, to give up. "Come on, come on, come on..." he muttered hoping beyond hope he was strong enough to keep them safe. That's when the storm decided he too would be taken. When Yuen's feet left the ground, his heart stopped. His life flashed before his eyes. His family, his career, and his sister whom he would never see again.

He felt a sudden firm grip on his ankles. Peering down, he saw it was Rylon. The Borgan stomped each of his feet, breaking through the floor to anchor himself against the raging storm. Clovis biting at his robes and pulling in some valiant attempt at helping. All around was chaos. Nothing but death and destruction, with Garrison and

Brotherhood fleeing for their lives or desperately searching for somewhere safe. In the midst of it all, Desmond's unconscious body was gently moved by the wind, cradled like a precious gem. He was placed underneath the altar of the Monastery where nothing could hurt him. Trisk looked downwards to the others. The newly met Borgan was holding them in place for the moment, but this reprieve wouldn't last long. That much he was sure of.

"I knew I should have stayed in the Library" Trisk muttered under his breath. His vison went white as a massive bolt of lightning forked mere inches passed him and struck the ground just a foot away from Rylon, blinding him for a second. Trisk peered up into the Galomorick when his sight returned. Through thundering rain and flashing lightning, Trisk could just about make out a figure in the centre of it all. His wide grey eyes met the eyes of the figure of shadows. Colour meeting void. Life meeting death.

Then, as soon as it began, the storm seemed to

fold in on itself losing its momentum. Trisk and the others crashed back to the floor in a long line letting out various groans of pain in the process. Yuen being the loudest with him landing on his prior injury. Only Rylon remained standing and that had been by sheer will alone.

"Is - Is it over...?" Mari asked gingerly, too afraid to lift her head to check for herself.

Seeing the black cloud begin to dissipate, A let out a long sigh of relief "I think so"

Laughing at the absurdity of what they had just suffered and survived, Mari laid on the floor limps spread like a sea star on the coral reefs "Rosylin would have a field day over this" out of the rubble of what was left of the ancient building, what remained of Urdel's men and the surviving Brothers wandered their way back into the light. Some wounded, all clearly rattled but grateful to be alive.

Then Urdel reappeared with a crash as loud as the thunder was. The Borgan threw off the fallen rocks and wooden beams that had fallen on him when the celling collapsed. Blood caked his forehead and his left arm had been crushed in the accident. His shoulders shook not from fear but with fury. Suddenly, his wild eyes were fixed on A. "You…" he seethed viciously "This is all your fault"

The Half-Breed rolled his eyes raising to his feet. Trisk, Mari, and Yuen following suit. "You're blaming me for this?" he said with a scoff "You know, I've been blamed for some stupid stuff over the years, but the weather has to be a first"

"If you had just taken your punishment like a real man, I wouldn't even be here to drag you back, you Gods damned freak of nature!" the thunder rumbled once more, setting everyone on edge. Some men didn't even hesitate and rushed for the exit.

Rylon stepped behind A, meeting his brother eye to eye "Urdel, enough. Half your men are dead. The other half are either injured or escaping as we speak" he said pointing behind Urdel.

Urdel's face was almost purple when he saw his men who had once been so loyal were now abandoning him for their own safety. "Get back here!" he ordered but no one listened or even paused. "Fine..." he turned back to his target "Maybe Lord Callum will pay me extra for bringing you to him single handedly"

A tensed reaching for his blades which had miraculously remained in his possession during the storm. Rylon placed a firm hand on A's shoulder engulfing it entirely. "There has been enough death today, brother. Leave on your own accord before I do something I'll regret"

His brother's gaze turned cold as ice "Was that a threat? Are you threatening me, little brother? Oh, you are going to regret that" Urdel raised his good arm to punch but the strike never came. Tunnel wind swept Urdel off his feet and was ripped out of the Monastery with a shout. Rain began to pour down once again, this time stronger than ever.

"Not again..." Mari whined

"Let's not stick around for round two" A huffed sweeping Clovis into his arms "let's go"

Yuen nodded "You heard the man. Everyone out!" he ordered the remaining soul inside the ruined building. Outside, just outside the gates of Marden, Lord Callum and his men stared at the growing chaos in utter shock and disbelief. Never before had they seen a storm cause such carnage. Nor had they seen one build back up so quickly in such a short space of time.

Shaking his head, Lord Callum turned around "Call the retreat" he said to his nearest officer. "No chance he'll survive that"

The officer paused "But Sir, the people -"

"Not our problem. You can't fight nature" Callum stated walking away from Marden. The Officer gave the signal, and the gathered forces began the long trek home. Ignoring the seams and cries for help of the Marden people. Unaware that a certain Prince had seen them retreat from his window in the jailhouse.

Running outside, A and the others saw the Galomorick Storm's devastation with their own eyes. The Monastery had only escaped complete destruction by a thread. The rest of Marden hadn't fared so well. The howling winds had made the mist vanish, allowing them to see the city entirely. "Creator's mercy..." Trisk mumbled with a heavy heart. There was no telling how many were dead. How many were trapped. How many had escaped. "Those poor people"

Marden had been practically decimated. Barely any buildings remained in one piece and those still standing were left without roofs or shaken to their foundations. Figures of dazed and confused citizens wandered the rubble strewn streets clawing at fallen stone or shouting for their loved ones. Echoes of people trapped floated on the wind.

Yuen stood hunched beside A, trying his best to ignore his injury "We need to evacuate. Before this Storm gets any worse" as the words left his mouth, a thunderous, tremendous roar vibrated the very stairs they stood upon. All in the vicinity looked up once more, up at the Storm that had reeked such havoc.

The Galomorick was changing. The person Trisk had spotted in the centre of it all let out a pained cry, shadowy hands clutching at his head and mouth agape in a roaring scream, as if in physical pain. Lightning flashed once more with the brightness of the sun itself. Four massive thuds followed in succession followed by tremble of the ground.

Before them stood a mighty Wolf. Made of swirling winds, stormy black clouds, flashing lighting and rumbling thunder. The fallen rubble made for its fangs and two glowing white orbs that crackled with unbridled power made for its eyes. The Galomorick Strom had taken its final form.

Pandamonium ensued.

"Oh, bloody hell" A whispered unable to look away from the monster in the sky. The Galomorick's eyes fixed above them, orbs turning into glowing slits as it snarled thunderously.

The staircase beneath their feet crumbled away

as hurricane strength winds engulfed the area. Trisk, Mari, Yuen, and Rylon fell with one part of the staircase while A remained on the other which was being sucked into the sky along with what was left of the Monastery of Astrid.

"A!!" Trisk screamed reaching out his hand but A, thinking fast, threw Clovis at him at the last second. A was then gone in a matter of seconds into the storm. The section of marble staircase he had been on swallowed by the mouth of the Galomorick "NO!" the Kaligan cried, heart clenching in terror at the fate of his companion.

Lost in the storm, A used his twin blades as an anchor in the marble and hung on for dear life. He could barely see through the pelting rain or screaming winds. He wasn't the only one trapped in a nightmare. Several citizens of Marden had become trapped in the storm just like him, screaming and crying and begging the Gods for mercy. One young woman screamed frantically as she was flung past him. A managed to grab her by the arm whilst his other hand clung to the blade's handle as tight as he could.

"Don't let me go!" she pleaded, bright green hair blowing wildly

"I won't let you go!" A responded even though his grip on her was slipping. Sadly, he couldn't hold onto her for long and she slipped from his hold."Help me!" her cry echoed as she vanished from his sight. A felt a surge of regret and closed his eyes sadly.

Back on the ground, the Galomorick gazed upon the remains of Marden, of its innocent people who had died. It wasn't satisfied. It would never be satisfied. Not until he had suffered his rightful fate. With that settled, the Galomorick's glowing orbs scanned the crumbling city, jetting from soul to soul until, at last, it found its intended target. Captain Urdel of Riven.

Like a coward, Urdel had tried to flee when the Galomorick had pulled him from A and the others but found his route of escape blocked. Urdel had studied Marden long before he had laid his trap. Or more specifically, Marden's mountainside Monastery. Urdel was aware of a secret passageway built into the mountain that led deep, deep underground where no Storm could reach him. All he needed was to get there. And so, with a crushed arm and a suspected head injury, Urdel clambered his way up the mountainside on its perilous unmarked path.

Meanwhile, Rylon led the charge in the rescue of those who could still be saved. In mere minutes, he had gathered what was left of Marden's armed forces to help dig out trapped individuals and carry out those who couldn't walk. Yuen, Mari, and Trisk aided where they could. The Galomorick was slowly making its way towards the still standing mountain which gave them at least some precious time to get people to safety. Clovis would run ahead and bark loudly at places where people were trapped. "Good boy, Clovis" Mari told him petting his soaked fur "Over here!" she would then shout to alert the others.

Back with A, the gravity of his predicament was quickly setting in. He had no escape, no way to fight. His death was surely on its way. Another screaming voice got his attention. Peering through the rain, A caught sight of the Kaligan Prince from earlier. His golden circlet long gone letting his pale hair fly madly in the swirling storm. He reached out for A like the woman before and like before, A managed to grab him by his arm.

"Not again" he grunted, using all his strength to pull the Prince up to the marble where the Prince gladly grasped one of the blade handles.

The Prince gasped "Thank you so much, you saved me, thank you!" he didn't seem to register that A was a Half-Breed in that moment. Or given their situation, didn't care. A wasn't going to bring it up.

"Don't thank me yet" the Half-Breed responded as lightning forked right past them

The Prince turned his head out of instinct. When he did, he spotted something curious bellow them "What is that?" he asked getting a to look as well. Bellow them, at the heart of the Galomorick storm, was the man made of shadows that Trisk had spotted earlier.

A's light blue eyes widened to the size of saucers. "Crosses paths with an angry spirit…" he mumbled remembering Cassadore's earlier warning "That's it" he said louder "We need to get down there. Take that thing down"

The Prince gawked at him like he was crazy "Are you insane!?"

"Would you rather just wait for whatever might happen to us?" A retorted

"No, but…" the Kaligan floundered for words "What if you make thing worse?"

A huffed pulling himself onto the chunk of marble fully, prying one blade free as he did "Do not lose that" before the Kaligan could even think of something to say to convince him not to attempt such a mad endeavour, A had already jumped.

* * *

Mari could hear the sobbing of a child. Running towards the sounds, she found a small boy no older than four stuck atop the rickety remains of his home. He was crying loudly, clutching a sopping wet blanket as the wooden beams of his house swayed dangerously. "Hang on, I'm coming!" she called up to him. Mari wasn't that good of a climber, but determination made her movements good enough to reach the boy "It's alright. It's alright, I've got you" she picked the boy up into her arms where he kept sobbing for his mother. There was no sign of her around so Mari could only assume the worst. One of the wooden beams snapped and the whole structure collapsed with Mari and the little boy still atop it.

She turned her body to take the full brunt of the fall, the boy clutched tightly in her arms, but the pain of hitting the ground never came. "Got you!" Yuen gasped catching her just in time.

"Thank you" she said gratefully with a smile in

his direction. Their eyes met for the first time. Gold and Onyx. "Um... hi"

"Hi..." Yuen breathed finding himself smiling as well.

The little boy started to cry once more which brought them back to their senses. They rejoined the survivors at the gates whereby some miracle, the boy's mother was waiting for him. He was swept out of Mari's arms and into the loving embrace of his weeping mother.

High above on the mountainside, Urdel struggled to hold onto the slippery rocks with only one functioning arm. Still, he persevered. Determined to get to the tunnel and to safety. The fate of the men who he had dragged halfway across the country for this set up didn't even cross his mind.

He let out a grunt as he moved from one stone to another, pausing for a moment to gather his bearings. His heart fell when a gust of ice-cold air hit his back. Slowly, he turned his head where he was met with the two glowing orbs of the Galomorick Storm.

Inside the creature, the Kaligan Prince watched in utter disbelief as the Half-Breed he had just met plummet towards the heart of the Storm. "Creators above, grant this man a swift death if nothing else" he prayed not even humouring the idea that A could succeed in his task. As for A, the closer he got to the shadowy figure, the more he was regretting his choices.

"Here goes nothing" he muttered as he drew ever closer. The shadow let out a furious cry when A crashed on top of him. Arms wrapped around the figure's throat for a steady hold. Outside, Urdel watched in terror as the Galomorick roared in his face pinned him to the mountain by the face of the wind escaping its mouth.

All A had on him as means of attack was one of his blades gifted by the people of TeraKyla. He wasn't even sure it would work but it was better than nothing. With one arm still wrapped around the shadow's throat, A stabbed the shadow where his torso would be if he was human. The figure wailed in agony, where A had stabbed him now glowing as white as the Galomorick's glowing orbs. To the survivors, the creature appeared to tremble

"It's working?" A asked himself in disbelief "It's working" with renewed vigour, A stabbed the shadow again and again wherever he could reach. Granting the Galomorick a second death with every fell of the blade. Outside, the Galomorick howled, roared, wailed. Its body shaking and shifting with every stab at its heart. The shadow figure, still burning with the desperate fires of anger and revenge, tried desperately to shake A off him. Clawing at his arm and face for any sort of purchase. In response,

A grabbed at the shadow, forcing it to face him. With the glowing light emanating from his injuries, A could make out the pained face of what was once a Pangarian man. The man whose spirit had crossed paths with the Storm.

A felt a twinge of sympathy, only a twinge, as he embedded the blade one final time with a mighty cry into the chest of the spirit. Exactly where his heart used to beat.

The Galomorick Storm let out one last growling howl to the sky, filled with all the pain and betrayal the spirit had felt during its last moments alive. With that, the wolf form the Strom had taken crashed into the mountainside with what was left of its physical form. Creating an unstoppable rockslide towards the survivors. "RUN!" Rylon ordered pointing frantically to the gates. An avalanche of rocks cascaded down towards the remains of Marden crushing anything in its path.

While the others fled for their lives, Mari was frozen in place. Her fear overcame her making her unable to move. It was only when the rocks tumbled over what was left of the grand staircases did Trisk realise she hadn't run with them. "Mari!" he screamed turning on his heel to go back for her. Yuen in tow rushing to aid the woman.

Wide-eyed Mari remained rooted in place her legs unable to move a fraction other than to tremble where she stood. Suddenly, Mari's instincts finally kicked in and she screamed. But not just any scream of terror. This scream was different

It was an ear-piercing, drum-breaking, all-encompassing shriek that exploded from the golden-haired woman's mouth. Both Trisk and Yuen fell to their knees covering their ears from the sudden onslaught of noise. The cascade of rocks which should have rightly killed all three of them crumbled to dust the instant they came within the vicinity of her scream. With her voice like no other, Mari effectively stopped the avalanche in its tracks saving those who were left alive. She finally stopped screaming when the rocks ceased to fall. Mari collapsed to her knees her chest heaving. She appeared shaken at what she had just done. "Well... never done that before"

❋ ❋ ❋

"Hey? Hey, are you alright?" the prince asked appearing in his line of sight. A had only regained consciousness a few seconds previously after dealing the final blow to the heart of the storm.

A groaned "I've been better" The other man held out his arm for A. A took it and allowed him to pull A to his shaky feet. The sky rapidly began to clear back to its normal bright daylight and the rain had stopped falling altogether. "What a mess" he commented at the devastation all around them.

"Maybe, but at least we got to live to see it" the Prince said with a smile

A shook his head "I wish I had your optimism"

"I wish I had your bravery. That was incredible what you did"

Around them, those who had been trapped in the Galomorick alongside them walked or limped towards them. Including the woman A had failed to save earlier. Among them, walking noticeably disorientated, was Desmond. The last of Urdel's men who had remained in the Monastery. "What the hell happened out here?" he demanded but the strength in his voice fell flat. He looked passed A and the Prince and let out a gasp of what could only be described as heartbreak.

Behind them stood the fading spirit of Rei.

"Rei..." Desmond said stumbling forward "I knew it. I knew I should have checked. Rei, my... my dearest Rei, forgive me. Please forgive me" the man pleaded falling to his knees in tears. Rei's spirit smiled warmly at his friend. No sign of anger or pain on his young face. He patted Desmond on his head, phantom fingers moving as if to ruffle his hair. The spirit lifted his head to meet the gaze of A. He saluted in respect with his arm across his chest. His respect, his gratitude. With that, the spirit faded out of sight. With his second death, Rei's soul was no longer consumed by rage or betrayal. He could now pass on peacefully.

"Was he your friend?" asked the Prince

Desmond nodded shakily "Urdel, he - my Captain killed him some days ago. He lied to me.

Said Rei had returned home sick. I'm such an idiot" Desmond seethed "I should have known. I should have checked. Why didn't I check?"

From behind the pair, A collapsed to the floor

Near the gates, Trisk rubbed one of his pointed ears while asking "What... was that?"

She laughed awkwardly "Um... is now a bad time to say I'm technically part Siren?"

"You're a what?" Yuen said wide eyed

"Only like, one sixteenth" she defended "Seriously, it's nothing that you need to -"

Appearing some several feet up the hill of fallen debris, a woman with wild green hair waved her arms for their attention. "Over here, quick! He needs help!"

"Oh, thank the Four, more survivors" Rylon said with relief palpable in his voice. Out of nowhere, Clovis bounded up the hill barking like mad. Trisk was the first to follow the puppy up the hill. "Over here. This way" the green-haired Pangarian woman urged Trisk to follow her. Trisk did so only to nearly faint when he saw what was ahead of him.

A was among the survivors but he was badly wounded. "Oh no... A!" he gasped breaking into a run.

Behinds him, hearing the news, Mari and Yuen were quick to follow suit with Rylon close behind. "A's alive!?" Mari choked on her own disbelief as she hurried after him. She too was nearly brought to her knees once more at the state of her companion "Oh my gods..."

Clovis whimpered nudging his head against A's leg but the Half-Breed barely reacted. He was close to passing out from blood loss at that point so he could barely focus on the people above him or what they were saying.

Everything hurt. He couldn't think straight. His eyesight began to darken while the companions he had met these last few weeks argued and panicked over how to help him. "Stay with us, A!" he vaguely heard someone tell him.

Sweet darkness overcame him, and A felt

nothing at all.

CHAPTER SIXTEEN

Where it all Started

He woke up slowly. The lull of sleep still grasping at his senses. He scrunched his eyes at the sunlight bleeding in through the large open windows. He would have gone back to sleep happily had a shock of pain from the slightest movement hadn't shot up his body from navel to collarbone. A huffed through the pain, opening his eyes once more. That was when he realised where he was. Much to his confusion, A found himself lying in a grand four poster bed propped up with soft pillows and tucked under a warm blanket. The bedroom his was situated in was also just as grand with ornate furniture decorated with gold and ivory.

It was most definitely; the strangest place A had

ever woken up in.

With great difficulty he lifted his arm to pull the blanket up to check his injuries. Furthering his confusion, his chest and torso was bandaged up in clean white bandages and the cuts on his arm had been tended to as well. Someone had gone out of their way to care for him. This fact alone was enough to make his head spin.

The door to the bedroom opened. A tensed, glancing at the window as a means of escape should the worst happen. Entering the room was Trisk carrying a tray of food on a platter. The Kaligan all but yelped when he saw A was awake, dropping the tray in the process "He's awake!" he yelled into the corridor "Guys! Guys, A's awake!"

"Trisk?" the Half-Breed questioned a split second before the Kaligan practically threw himself on A in a tight hug. "Trisk - Trisk, ow!" he exclaimed forcefully which made Trisk leap away out of fear of causing further damage.

The Kaligan smiled apologetically "Sorry, sorry.

I'm just so happy you're awake. We were starting to worry you'd never wake up"

"A!" Mari's excited shout from the door cut through the air. The golden-haired Pangarian grinned brightly coming towards them "Thank goodness. You gave us the fright of a lifetime back there. I was certain you were done for"

At the doorway, Yuen chuckled "He's a fighter. I'll give him that" the Guard leaned against the doorway with one arm in a sling and sporting a few new cuts on his face. Both Mari and Trisk had some fading bruises and some minor cuts but were otherwise unharmed. "If you're ever in need of employment, I'd be happy to recommend you for the Royal Guard. They could use a man like you"

A just looked at them all puzzled "...What are you talking about?"

Mari started to frown "Do you not remember?"

The Half-Breed shrugged "It's a bit of a blur, honestly. Last thing I remember is getting caught in that thing. Then waking up here"

"Probably for the best you don't recall. Cylassan told us how terrifying it must have been inside the Galomorick" A glanced at Trisk not knowing who he was speaking about "Oh, Prince Cylassan. He says you saved his life"

Looking at the Half-Breed, Mari bit back her laugh at how utterly baffled A was at the news "I did what now?"

"Where do you think you are right now?" a fifth voice joined in entering the bedroom. Cylassan walked towards the bed with Rylon behind him. The Borgan smiled at A and gave a polite wave. In his arms lay a sleeping Clovis. Cylassan came to a stop just before A's bedside. He took a kneeling position, bowing his head in respect. "I am pleased to see you have rejoined us in the waking world. Please, accept my most sincere gratitude for your daring defeat of the Galomorick Storm. I am in your debt, good Sir. On behalf of the Havenfall family, welcome to Ryu"

Slowly, A turned his gaze to Trisk "How - How long was I out for?"

"About two weeks" he answered "Prince Cylassan ensured you get only the best care for your heroics as he put it"

Cylassan laughed lightly "It was the least I could do" he got back to his feet. In Rylon's arms, Clovis yawned as he woke up. In a flash, he was out of the Borgan's arms and on the bed licking A's face with boundless excitement and happy yips. A winced when Clovis put his paws on his chest.

"Wait, two weeks?" he asked after prying Clovis off his face "It took us two weeks to get to Marden and that was with delays"

Seeing where A was going, Cylassan answered his unasked question "Simple, really. We took the Lambs Grove trail. It cut our journey down by a week"

"Oh. Did it now?" A said sarcastically giving Trisk an incredibly pointed look

Trisk let out a nervous chuckle "Yeah... turns out you were right about that shortcut" A smacked Trisk's arm only to regret it instantly as the pain hit again.

"We should leave him to rest" Rylon said finding the interaction quite amusing "The Half-Breed has been through quite the ordeal"

Prince Cylassan made a disgusted face "We must come up with a better name than that. Makes the man sound like an animal. Perhaps we can just address him by his name?"

"Ah, about that" Mari said glancing at A not sure whether to say it or not.

A sighed "I don't have one. Never got one. Just call me A"

The Prince became openly shocked "You... don't have a name?" he asked quietly, and A nodded wordlessly "I apologise. I had no idea" he averted his gaze "We'll leave you to rest" Cylassan then made a hasty exit out of embarrassment. One by one they left A to continue his rest in the cozy bed and fluffy pillows. All but Clovis who refused to budge from A's bed. He curled up beside A on the bed, his breathing becoming slow as he drifted off to sleep.

A wasn't sure what to think. He wasn't sure about anything at all. All his life, he'd received nothing but scorn and disgust for simply being born. His heritage was not something he could control and yet he had paid the price since birth. Not even having Overtime, A had grown used to the harsh glares, the whispered glances, the open hostility. It was all he had ever known. It was why he had kept to himself all these years. He'd tried in the past to make friends, find companionship, but at every turn his efforts were in vain. A had accepted that he would be alone till his dying day.

Then he crossed paths with a Scan from the Redencon Library on a search to make history for himself. There had been times when A wondered why he hadn't ditched Trisk that first night in the forest. Why he hadn't just walked away while Trisk slept and been done with the Kaligan he'd unwillingly picked up in Ryu? At the very least he would have avoided getting sucked into a Galomorick storm, however fuzzy those memories might be.

Afterwards was Mari. Another chance encounter A shouldn't have made if things had gone according to his original plan. She had seen him as a person, not a Half-Breed. For the first time in years, somebody looked at him with kindness and not the usual disregard for his existence. It should have made A happy. Instead, it left him with the feeling of a stone in his stomach. He was far from someone who could openly trust another. In truth A didn't want to trust any of them. Far too many bad experiences to count had taught A well enough that trust was a mug's game that would only end with him alone getting hurt. But Mari's genuine attempts at friendship made A want to try. And that scared him.

He Barely knew of Yuen. Hardly spoke to him during or after the events at TeraKyla. Yet the Pangarian man who had no connection to the forsaken town had risked everything to protect it against almost impossible threats. A could respect that kind of bravery. Maybe that's what inspired him to join in the fight. Or maybe it was Aaron's senseless death hitting too close to home that made him want to fight. Both options left A questioning many things he had once been so sure of.

Lastly, there was Rylon. The very reason A ended up in this unfairly comfy bed. The Borgan had been the epitome of what a Borgan should be. Gentle and giving with a dedication to helping others. Even though his background was questionable to say the least, Rylon hadn't hesitated to stand before Urdel and demand he leave A and the others alone. Even going so far as to offer protection under his Order. A still couldn't wrap his head around that. Why even bother? A was as good as dead when Urdel arrived. What was the point of sticking his neck out for someone like him?

As A mused to himself on these confusing conflicting thoughts. Clovis snuggled up against him letting out an almost sigh of contentment. A unconsciously started to pet the dog. Stroking his soft abundant fur through his fingers. He let out his own exhale through the nose, tilting his head to look down at the once again sleeping dog. A's brow furrowed "Is it me or are you getting bigger?" with no answer from the puppy, not that he'd get one, A let out a long yawn. His exhaustion came back tenfold. Maybe another nap was needed. It would be a shame to waste such a nice bed after all. A was asleep within moments, one hand resting on Clovis's sleeping back.

The Half-Breed slept for another three days before being able to get out of bed. Trisk later explained to him that he had technically died twice on the route back to Ryu. Only surviving thanks to Rylon being an impressively talented healer. A was somewhat glad he remembered next to nothing of that time frame. Once he was back on his feet and able to walk unaided, Cylassan made the bold choice to demand an audience with his father. The current Kaligan King.

It was no secret that their relationship was

strained to the point of breaking. The fact that Cylassan was King Alexius's only legitimate son was the only reason the Prince had yet to be disowned and banished. Alexius had arrived in Ryu only a few days prior to A waking up after learning his son was back in the city. He was informed of the Galomorick Storm and of how his son was lucky to survive. Tales of the heroics shown that day were spanning all four corners of Endonia, and Alexius was not amused in the slightest.

"Enter" he announced after hearing someone knock on the door. He was situated in one of the more luxurious offices the building had to offer and sat behind a desk made of meridian stone found only in the most southern reaches of Endonia. Cylassan stepped inside with a composure that did not reach his eyes. Cylassan took after his mother appearance wise.

His features softer and kinder than his father. However, this only made the tension between them worse as the marriage between his parents was tumultuous before she died which had bled into his relationship with his father.

"Hello, Father. I wish to have a word with you if I may"

The elder Kaligan gestured for him to take a seat "Since when do you ask permission from me to speak?" he commented "Go on then. What is it that you want?"

Cylassan bit his tongue to keep a level head. His father's dismissive tone never ceased to rattle him "As you know, I was almost killed in the Marden disaster. I was one of the lucky few to have made it out of that nightmare alive, thanks to those who were there that day"

"Ah, yes. That lot" Alexius said with a frown "I hope you're here to tell me this charity case you're doing has run its course. I've grown tired of bumping into them in the hallways. Especially that freak you insisted get treated by the Havenfall's private doctors. At our expense no less"

The vein in Cylassan's forehead throbbed "I

think you mean the man who saved my life and practically took down that Storm all on his own?" Alexius waved his words off and Cylassan took a deep breath "As I was saying, I'm here to make a proposal. One I think you will find very interesting"

Alexius peeked at his son over the rims of his spectacles "Oh, this I have to hear"

"I'm sure your well aware of their exploits by now. Not just about what happened in Marden. I propose we capitalise on this opportunity" he explained with a hopeful look

His father removed his glasses to rub his eyes "If you're suggesting what I think you're suggesting, you can stop right now" the older announced replacing his glasses back on his nose "I will not have you turn those bunch of ruffians into a publicity stunt for us. Creators know our Family name is damaged enough as it is"

"Well, I'm not the one who led the army" Cylassan muttered mockingly. He then let out a put-upon sigh with slumped shoulders to boot "Well, it was just an idea. Just thought we should get ahead of this before the Pangarians do"

That caught Alexius's attention. The man set down the paper he was holding and rested his chin on his hands "Elaborate"

Cylassan shrugged again "I'm just saying, two members of these 'ruffians' as you called them are Pangarian. It wouldn't be a stretch to assume the Camire Family would also jump at the opportunity to claim them for Endonia" Cylassan shook his head "Ah, but what do I know? Apologies for the interruption, Father"

he stood from his seat, bowing at his father as an act of respect. Cylassan hadn't even made it near the door before Alexius spoke again.

"You… raise a valid point" he admitted reluctantly after thinking it over "It would be… prudent to take this opportunity while we still can. What do you suggest?"

Cylassan allowed himself to coyly smile while his back was turned to his father. "I have a few ideas.

We'll have to get the word out before anything else. Just leave it to me"

The older Kaligan stared at him with mounting suspicion "I have your best friend killed, and you haven't done anything in response to that. Anyone else would be frothing at the mouth with the need for revenge. Tell me boy, where is that anger you've always held towards me? I barely recognise you as my son when you act like a fallen doe during a hunt"

The Prince willed himself to keep calm. He couldn't afford his emotions to run free just yet. No, he would never forgive his father for what he did to his Tharian. Not as long as he drew breath. But his father would never know that. Instead, Cylassan broke the silence between them "Let's just say facing death head on makes one re-evaluate one's priorities. Have a pleasant evening, Father"

Alexius found himself chuckling to himself as Cylassan walked away "Well, look at that. There's some sense in you after all" his son, with his back turned on his father, scowled as he left the office, forcing himself to close the door and not slam it shut like he wanted to.

Outside the office he paused to collect himself. Becoming the steadfast, dependable Prince Ryu knew and loved once again. With that settled, Cylassan went to fetch his horse from the stables outside. There was work to be done.

In the coming days, Cylassan ensured the news spread as far as word of mouth and paper could travel. From the Mountainous regions of the north to the desert cities of the south. Soon enough all of Endonia was aware of the events of what happened in Marden.

At Mari's old campsite, the news reached them quickly in the form of official news written on paper known as a gazette "Rosilyn! Rosilyn!" one of the woman's campmates cried running towards her, paper in hand "Look! Look, it's about Mari!"

Rosilyn dropped her needlework without thinking and snatched the paper from the other's hand. She read the gazette paper, eyes growing wide as tears of pride welled "That girl" she whispered shaking her head in fondness "That wonderful, crazy girl"

It reached the Library of Redencon by way for messenger bird "Hey Drannor, have you seen this yet?" asked Trisk's past roommate, handing the other Scan his copy of the gazette paper he just received. Drannor paused his work to see what his friend was on about. The splutter that escaped his throat filled the room.

"You're kidding me" he said with a smile "He did it. Ha! Son of a banshee, he actually did it!" with true happiness for their friend who had left to follow his dreams, the two Scans couldn't help but break out the wine after pinning the copy onto the Library's notice board.

Near a quaint mossy lake in a simple but comfortable wooden house, the greying Pangarian woman came into the house with tears in her eyes "Darling look. It's our Yuen. He's a hero" she said beaming with joy handing the paper over to her husband. The man quickly read the paper, his hands shaking as the words sank in.

"What in Endonia's name is a Galomorick?" he asked half confused but still bursting with admiration towards his son's actions "Well, we can certainly say our boy does nothing by halves"

His wife snickered "Wonder where he gets it from"

※ ※ ※

For the most part, King Alexius had been left in the dark about Cylassan's plan. All he knew was his son planned on using the events at Marden to their advantage and that was frankly all he cared about. So long as Cylassan succeeded in helping the Havenfall image to the people, he didn't care about the smaller details. That was until he discovered the Ryu Palace's ballroom being decorated for a grand affair. Only then did Alexius start asking questions. Cylassan wasn't only claiming the group for the Kaligans. He was making them official representatives of the Kaligan Crown.

The King could have passed away then and there from sheer outrage alone. How dare his son do this behind his back. He had half a mind to go through with the banishment once and for all but realised Cylassan had played it smart and had backed him into a corner. Should Alexius call off the ceremony, the Pangarians would no doubt see this as an act of weakness on his part. Proof that King Alexius was unwilling to embrace the peace between races he so often claimed to support once the war had ended.

He had to give Cylassan credit. His son could be a conniving pain in the neck when he wanted to be

As for A and the others, all they had been told was that Cylassan was hosting a celebration in honour of the fallen of Marden. He hinted to a reward of some kind to the five who were paramount in saving lives but that was it. They were given new clothes to wear made of the finest fabrics. "Seems like a lot to go through for a memorial service" commented Mari while she marvelled at her new dress. Gold to match her hair

"He did mention a reward. Maybe this is what he meant?" offered Trisk with a shrug

A flipped the hood up on his new cloak to hide his ears. After weeks of not being able to cover himself like he used to, it was nice to return to a sense of normalcy.

Soon enough, the throne room of Ryu's palace filled with eager guests from all over Endonia for the ceremony. Some familiar faces filled the audience. Rosilyn had come as well as Jask though the two would never meet. Several citizens of TeraKyla and Elayas were in attendance with Langnir among them standing proudly at the back to allow others to see unobstructed. Most important were the survivors of Marden who had gladly spread the word about the five's efforts and heroics on that terrible day. Cylassan had them all transported to Ryu as refugees since Marden would most likely never be rebuilt after such devastation.

Unbeknownst to A who could not read or write,

the gazette piece Cylassan had authored painted him as the valiant hero who selflessly defeated the Galomorick Storm singlehandedly while his companions saw to the rescue efforts. He had no clue that his life would completely change from that day on. He and the other four stood at the front of the audience, dressed in the new clothing they had been given.

Trumpets blaring signalled the beginning of the ceremony. King Alexius made his entrance first flanked by armoured soldiers, followed behind by the Kaligan Council. Though he tried to hide it, his smile was strained from what he was forced to deal with for the sake of his reputation

Next to enter were some members of the extended Havenfall Family. Cylassan was the heir apparent, but he was not the only family Alexius had. Each donned in their best regalia, the family walked gracefully down the isle of the throne room towards Alexius. He took his seat on the throne while the Family stood on either side. Acting as a symbol of a united front when that was far from the truth.

Last to enter was Prince Cylassan himself. Unlike his father before him, his smile was a genuine one. He was enjoying this, and his father's unease more than he probably should. When he reached the front of the room he did not take his seat next to his father like he normally would. Today, Cylassan would take the lead. The music died off and Cylassan addressed the audience.

"My fellow citizens of Endonia" he began "Today we gather to mourn the loss of our brothers and sisters in Marden. The disaster that struck our nation has left us all reeling with shock and grief. Our hearts go out to the families and friends of those who lost their lives, and to those who have been injured or left homeless," he paused to let allow the audience to understand the depth of his words.

"We must honour the memory of those who have been lost by coming together as a nation and working towards a better future. We must rebuild what has been destroyed, and we must do so with compassion and empathy for those who have suffered. Therefore, it is with great pride that I can say that we have found five such people that represent the best of Endonia. Who will both serve and protect us in our darkest hour"

In the audience, Mari whispered to Trisk "He wouldn't..."

"...He might" Trisk whispered back just as shocked as she was

Cylassan continued "I am proud to stand before you today, not only as your prince, but also as a grateful citizen of this great nation. These five souls have shown us what it truly means to be brave, to be selfless, and to be willing to put one's life on the line for the greater good" he then looked directly at them. His arm was outstretched as a gesture for them to come up to where he was standing.

With all eyes on them, Yuen was the first to walk forward. Emboldened by his courage, Mari and Trisk did the same who were then followed by

Rylon. A remained where he stood not moving an inch. Cylassan motioned for them to kneel, and the audience watched breathlessly as they did.

"I dub thee, Sir Yuen of Droscal" he announced tapping the man's shoulder with the edge of his sword. Behind him, Alexius gripped the armrests of his throne barely managing to keep up his facade.

"I dub thee, Sir Trisk of Redencon" he repeated the same motion on Trisk's shoulder

"I dub thee, Lady Mari of Othenal Forest" Cylassan was sure to be careful not to cut her bare shoulder

I dub thee, Sir Rylon of Riven" he announced, knowing Rylon would prefer that over Marden. Cylassan then turned his gaze towards A who hadn't moved an inch since they had been called upon. "Arise, good Sir. I will not let a good deed go unrewarded"

Swallowing back the overwhelming anxiety plaguing his senses, A obeyed the Prince and took a kneeling position beside Trisk. Without his permission, Cylassan pulled down the hood of A's cloak revealing his half-breed nature to all. Though the audience was aware that a Half-breed was among the group who had saved Marden, none of them had ever seen one until that point with many having thought that part of the story must have been fabricated. The resounding gasps filling the Throne room was enough to make him want to vomit out of stress alone, but Cylassan raised his hand to silence the audience.

"I dub thee, Sir A of Ryu" he announced with a tap of his sword. His announcement spoke volumes to the audience. Cylassan was granting A, a nameless Half-Breed with nothing to his own not just a title and standing, but a place in Ryu that would always belong to him. Not even the residing Lord of Ryu himself could argue against it. A stared at the floor in utter disbelief. He must be dreaming. Perhaps he had never woken up at all.

"From this day forward, I hereby dub you all protectors of our realm. Ryu will be proud to call you their champions. Long live Endonia!"

Silence lingered among the audience for longer than what most could consider comfortable. But slowly, the cheers began and only grew louder. Moved by Cylassan's speech and his acceptance of A and his companions, how could they not show their support?

"Long live Endonia!" they cheered "Long live Endonia! Long live Endonia!"

The newly proclaimed Protectors rose to their feet and faced the audience. None of them believed this was happening. Mari had a dazed smile on her face. Yuen was composed but baffled. Trisk waved not knowing what else to do. Rylon bowed his head towards the people.

And as for A, he gazed upon the applauding, his cheering crowd, his expression one of indescribable astonishment, and wondered just what else fate had in store for him.

CHAPTER SEVENTEEN

What Lies Ahead

After the Ceremony, the adjacent ballroom was host to a magnificent gala in honour of the newly dubbed Protectors. Cylassan had spared no expense in the decorations, food, or entertainment. Much to the growing ire of Alexius.

Still, the Kaligan King could take comfort in the fact that they had bested the Camire Family for a change. All around the citizens of Ryu and the refugees of Marden mingled with those who had travelled from distant corners of Endonia. For that night and that night alone, harmony rang out among the guests. Pangarians and Kaligans alike laughed and broke bread like they were old friends. As if the years of war, bloodshed, and hatred hadn't ravaged Endonia.

Watching from his seat beside his father, Cylassan nursed his wine knowing it was all an act. Just a pretence. One simple party wasn't enough to truly break away from the binds of hostility that still clung to the very fabric of his world. It would take more than that to mend the ties between his people and the Kaligans. Unlike his father and his father before him, Cylassan believed that peace was a dream that could be achieved.

The peace treaties signed after the war were just paper. Mere empty promises that could be broken at any moment should the powerful demand it. Meeting Tharian had changed everything for him. Showing him that everything he had been taught about the other race was wrong. He would change Endonia for the better. Build it from the ground up if need be. Only then would Tharian's death not be in vain.

Cylassan side-eyed his father, grey eyes brimming with unspoken anger that had built up since childhood. If all else failed, the Prince was not opposed to more violent measures should the need demand so.

Across the ballroom, Rosilyn surprised Mari from behind by wrapping her in a bear hug so tight it took her breath away. "Rosilyn?" Mari gasped shocked. She quickly turned around and hugged the older Pangarian woman back "What are you doing here?"

"Oh darling, I wouldn't have missed this for the world!" she responded with her pearly tooth-filled smile "I am so proud of you, Mari" She pulled away from the hug, taking Mari's hands in hers "To think. Ten years ago, you were a runt of a thing stumbling towards my caravan. Now look at you…" the woman sniffed as tears filled her eyes "Oh, I promised myself I wouldn't cry"

Mari smiled brightly at her praise "I have you to thank. You taught me so much over the years. Whatever they pay me for this Protector thing, I'll send it to you. As repayment for caring for me"

The older woman shook her head "Goodness, no. Don't even think about it. You dare send me even a coin and we'll have words" it was said in jest and they both knew it "You know," Rosilyn continued now cupping Mari's cheek "When you appeared in my life, I had no idea how much the Gods had blessed me. I may have never had children of my own, but you, my dear girl, are mine. Blood be damned" Mari burst into tears pulling Rosilyn into another tight hug.

"Thank you, Rosilyn. For everything"

Whilst in the middle of a conversation with some of Ryu's most prominent scholars who were desperate to learn the details of his travels with A, Trisk spotted Jask among the guests. He excused himself from the men, made his way through the guests and found Jask leaning against one of the ballroom pillars semi-obscured by the white and gold drapery. "Jask?"

The other man looked up from his cup, recognition in his eyes "Well who'd have thought it.

Great to see you again, Trisk. Scan of the Redencon Library. First class, right?" Trisk nodded "Damn, you've done well for yourself. You and that Half-Breed" he glanced over Trisk's shoulder "Speaking of which, where is he? Can't believe I never noticed he was a Half-Breed of all things"

Trisk laughed awkwardly at Jask's well-meaning if crude comments "Yeah, well..." the Scan took a look at the room but couldn't see A anywhere "A doesn't do well with crowds. I doubt you'll catch him tonight"

"Shame" Jask added taking a long gulp of his wine "Glad I caught you though. I was hoping to discuss business with you. Now that you're moving up in the world and all"

Trisk sighed crossing his arms "What do you want?"

"It's nothing I want. It's something you want" he stepped closer, voice going lower as he whispered in Trisk's ear "It's about Lord Callum. You translated his papers for me, remember?"

The Scan blinked, now understanding. "I see" Trisk responded "Let's talk in private, shall we? We wouldn't want prying ears to overhear this"

Jask let out a hearty laugh "I knew I liked you"

Langnir's booming laughter echoed as he regaled the tale to the enraptured attendees "It was a fight for the ages. Aw, you should have been there. Guard Yuen stood against the beast all on his own. He took him down in single combat. Not only that, but he was also fighting fit only days later"

Fighting fit was quite an exaggeration to Yuen who was listening from a distance. He still had phantom pains from his injuries dealt to him not just at TeraKyla but also at Maren. His body had been pushed to the limit and he had wound up passing out from the pain lot long after A. Luckily, he had woken up only hours later, while A remained unconscious for weeks. Meeting Langnir again at the Gala had been a surprise. Langnir had lifted the man off his feet all but swinging him around with a joyous exclamation. It caught the attention of people close by who then swarmed the Borgan Mayor when he began his tale.

Yuen didn't interrupt though. He just watched from a distance looking pleased.

"How are your accommodations keeping you?" Rylon asked in concern "Do you need anything? Anything at all"

The two Marden natives shook their heads "Rylon, you've done more than enough for us already. Ryu has been treating us well. You have nothing to worry about" the woman said, chuckling at his worry.

Her friend on the other hand frowned "I am sorry about your brother. I heard he didn't survive the Storm" Rylon's face shifted into grief. Urdel's body had been found days after the event. Though he knew it had been next to impossible for his brother to have survived, he had still hoped. Hoped that maybe after the Strom had passed, after the dust had settled, he and Urdel could speak like brothers again and not enemies.

It had been a foolish hope, he supposed. The extent of Urdel's crimes had come out thanks to Desmond discovering Rei's records. Rylon had done many things he regretted whilst a criminal, but Urdel had been worse. So much worse that Rylon could scarlessly believe it.

"Thank you for your condolences" he said to the two women, the soft smile on his face not reaching his eyes.

As the Gala continued well into the night, Trisk had scoured the Ballroom and failed to spot A anywhere. He tracked down Mari and asked her if she had seen their Half-Breed companion. She hadn't either. The two thought that maybe A had left for the night. Perhaps the crowds were too much for him and he had gone to find somewhere quiet. Still, they became worried when neither Yuen nor Rylon had seen him since the Ceremony ended.

"Is something wrong?" Cylassan asked walking over to them

"We seem to have lost our friend" Mari told him "You haven't seen A, have you?"

Cylassan nodded before pointing to the massive ornate glass doors that lead out to the Palace's royal balcony. "He's out there. Poor guy looked like he was going to faint earlier, so I told him he could go get some air"

"I'll go check" Trisk announced already heading towards the balcony's glass doors. The Scan noted that the balcony had been roped off from the rest of the Gala. Trisk stepped over the blue velvet rope then opened the widow by the handle. The balcony overlooked the entirety of Ryu. Night had fallen and the city had come alive with lights and music along with its infamous night market. There he found A.

A was perched on the stone railing of the balcony, hood down for a change with the breeze blowing his light blue locks. As soon as he heard the door latch go, he quickly pulled his hood up once more. "Oh, it's you" he said to Trisk in place of greeting "Figured you'd be the one to find me"

Trisk smiled coming towards him "Enjoying the party? Or is that a stupid question"

A rolled his eyes "What do you think?"

"Got it. Stupid question. Hey, I'm sorry about all this. Had I known this is what Cylassan meant by a reward, I'd have said something. Sorry you had to go through that"

The Half-Breed stared at him, brows furrowed and eyes sharp. He then sighed "I know. Not exactly used to having so much attention on me. Last time that happened, I got into a tavern brawl" he said with a smirk.

"I said I was sorry" Trisk said in defence "So, any thoughts on our new positions? You think if we jump off this balcony, we'll be long gone before they notice?" At that, A snorted. Something Trisk hadn't heard him do until then. He gestured for Trisk to look down from the balcony himself. "Bloody -!" Trisk exclaimed stumbling backwards "That is high. That is very, very high. Ooh, I think I've got vertigo"

A looked at him with his head tilted "Marden

didn't give you vertigo, but that drop does?"

"There was a lot going on, ok?"

The doors to the balcony opened once more. Out walked Mari, Yuen, and Rylon. Clovis had stayed in the care of the servants that night as Alexius refused to let the puppy come along. The puppy had responded to such a dismissal by peeing on his robed coat while his back was turned. "Hey, how are you doing?" inquired Mari moving to lean against the railing next to where A sat.

"I'm fine. I just needed some air" the Half-Breed said

She hesitated for a second before speaking "Look, whatever Urdel said about you, about Lord Callum, I don't believe any of it" A opened his mouth to speak "You don't have to say anything. All of us have skeletons in our closets. Myself included... What I'm saying is, if you say it was an accident, then it was an accident. We believe you"

"I looked into this Lord Callum fellow while you slept. Nasty piece of work from what I could tell"

Yun added "Whatever happened between you two, you can count on me to be there should he come for you"

"And me" declared Rylon

"And me" finished Trisk with a smile

A was, again, speechless. He stared at these people, practically strangers to him, ready to fight by his side. His mind raced; his emotions ran wild. There were a thousand and one things he wasn't to say, a thousand and one questions he wanted to ask but his words failed him. So instead, A nodded resolutely "Thank you. All of you"

Suddenly, Mari gasped "Look!" she said pointing to the clear night sky. The City of Ryu had become famous for countless exploits and accomplishments over the centuries. However, the thing the city was most famous for was the lights.

On the rare occasion, when the sky was clear and the conditions were just right, the night sky would become illuminated with the most beautiful lights that danced across the night sky. Made of every colour imaginable, the lights moved like the ribbons dancers would use during their routines. No one knew when the lights would appear, so to see them in person was considered lucky beyond measure. Mari gasped softly "They're beautiful..."

"They are indeed" Yuen whispered, his eyes drifting away from the lights and towards the golden-haired woman beside him. Her matching eyes glowing in the dazzling lights drawing him in. He averted his gaze almost instantly. Trisk and A were enraptured by the lights as well. Neither had seen them the last time they were in Ryu.

Mari grinned "Let's make a wish"

"A wish?" Rylon repeated curiously "You wish on stars, not lights"

"Then let's make a promise" she declared passionately "A promise to each other and ourselves. To commemorate our new positions in Ryu"

Yuen shrugged "Sounds like fun"

"I'll go first" Mari looked up to the lights once more, clasping her hands together "... I will perform for the Empire of Song" she vowed placing one hand onto the railing.

Soon, Rylon placed his much larger hand onto the railing as well "I will make up for my past misdeeds"

Trisk was next, proudly placing his palm down on the same railing "I will make the discovery of a lifetime"

Yuen placed his hand down also, his expression steady as he made his promise "I will find my sister"

That left A last but not at all least. They looked at him expectantly "I..." he thought back on the past few weeks against the last twenty-five years of his life. How so much had happened in such a short time. All because one man refused to leave his side. Filled with a determination he had never felt before then, A slammed his hand down next to Trisk, heart pounding in his chest "I'll prove my worth to all of Endonia!" he ended up shouting.

"So? Are we all in?" Mari asked. All nodded in agreement "Then from here on out, we are Endonia's

Protectors. To us!"

"To us!" they cheered breaking into laughter. Tomorrow, their new positions as Protecters of the Realm would begin. Tomorrow they will serve Endonia to the best of their collective abilities. In due time, these five souls so different yet so similar, would one day make their mark in history.

But that was a story for tomorrow.

Printed in Great Britain
by Amazon